WHEN LIBERTY DIES

RICK WOOD

© Copyright Rick Wood 2017

Cover Design by TheBookCoverDesigner.com

Edited by Russel McLean, Writer's Workshop

Copy-edited by LeeAnn, FirstEditing.com

No part of this book may be reproduced without express permission from the author.

Any likeness to any real person, living or dead, is entirely coincidental. Each character is a work of fiction.

ALSO BY RICK WOOD

The Sensitives:

Book One – The Sensitives

Book Two – My Exorcism Killed Me

Book Three – Close to Death

Book Four – Demon's Daughter

Book Five – Questions for the Devil

Book Six - Repent

Book Seven - The Resurgence

Book Eight - Until the End

Shutter House

Shutter House

Prequel Book One - This Book is Full of Bodies

Cia Rose:

Book One – After the Devil Has Won

Book Two – After the End Has Begun

Book Three - After the Living Have Lost

Chronicles of the Infected

Book One – Zombie Attack

Book Two – Zombie Defence

Book Three – Zombie World

Standalones:

When Liberty Dies

I Do Not Belong

Death of the Honeymoon

Sean Mallon:

Book One – The Art of Murder

Book Two – Redemption of the Hopeless

The Edward King Series:

Book One – I Have the Sight

Book Two – Descendant of Hell

Book Three – An Exorcist Possessed

Book Four – Blood of Hope

Book Five – The World Ends Tonight

Non-Fiction

How to Write an Awesome Novel

Thrillers published as Ed Grace:

The Jay Sullivan Thriller Series

Assassin Down

Kill Them Quickly

This book is dedicated to all those who have suffered prejudice because of recent political changes.

These people in power do not speak for all of us.

CHAPTER ONE

IMAGINE FOR A MOMENT, if you will, that you are a person.

Man or woman, rich or poor, boy or girl.

It doesn't matter — this could happen to any of you.

Imagine you have a large group of friends, as you may well do. You spend time with these friends, find yourself accepted, have them come visit your family, and your family visits them.

Imagine then, that one day, those friends decide that they don't want you to spend time with them anymore.

That someone who bears a vague similarity to you hurts someone like them.

Now your friends judge you by that person. Even fear you. They decide that you are no longer welcome. They decide your family are no longer welcome. Even though you feel like you shouldn't have to justify who you are to these so-called friends, you still try to show them that you are a good person.

Imagine then, that these friends not only judge you by these other people but use it to incite a hatred that makes them intolerable of everything about you. Every accent, cultural aspect, piece of history, smell, look, sound; everything about you, they now detest.

Imagine people set up a protest against your presence in the city that you live in. They claim they are defending their country. They don't see you as 'English' or 'British.' Because of their precisely aimed hatred, they don't include you in their definition of that society.

Imagine if this is something you face daily. The more multicultural the place, the more people resent you. They protest your presence in their country.

What happens when these protests become violent?

What happens when this violence spreads throughout an entire city? A city full of violent people with hatred toward anyone who looks, sounds, or is remotely like you. For reasons that have nothing to do with you.

Imagine if that violence came with a threat of death. Or torture.

Is that too much for you to be able to imagine?

Well, don't worry, you don't have to.

Just look outside your window.

———

Suniya sat back and surveyed what she had just written.

Is it too aggressive? she wondered.

She sighed. It was up to how her tutor would read it, of course.

She reread the title of her university assignment, trying to decide whether she had actually written a relevant answer or just random ramblings.

The psychology of racism – ingrained, or learned behaviour?

It was a loaded title.

She had answered the question, of course, she was sure of that. It was just... There were no references. No quotes, no bibliography. Surely it's a prerequisite of an assignment to back up your points with research.

But how are you supposed to reference the world around you?

She closed the Word document, inadvertently directing the screen to Google Chrome, where a YouTube video she had used as research resumed

A group of blokes pack themselves into a train on the underground. Given, they were squeezed in, but nevertheless, there is definitely room for one more.

And one more is trying to get on.

But these people won't let him.

Because he's black.

Every time this man tries to get back on the train, any attempt he makes to step on, this group of rowdy lads push him back off.

To add extra impetuous, as if the motive to their actions was not at all clear, each one of these lads is singing, "We're racist and we know it."

How am I supposed to quote this?

She let out another exasperated exhalation. She checked the time. Not long before she needed to meet Eric.

Eric, her boyfriend.

Her white boyfriend.

She a Muslim, he a white atheist.

She closed her eyes and imagined what would happen if these men on the train saw them together. Holding hands, strolling happily down the street. Cultures combined in mutual love.

Would they do more to hurt them than just sing them a song and push them off the train?

Not that singing racial chants and victimising someone in such a way is not horrific, of course.

Maybe this course wasn't such a good idea if such things make me so angry, she sniggered to herself. She was nearing the end of the first year of her degree in Philosophy and Psychology, specifically working on a module to do with the psychology of racial hatred.

She had worked so damn hard. Done everything she had to. More than others.

Because for some reason, I feel like I need to work harder than everyone else.

Right! Enough of this stupid thinking. The assignment was done. Don't want to be late.

She signed her name at the bottom:

Suniya Aisha Afaaq.

She closed her laptop, grabbed her coat, and caught sight of herself in the mirror. She tutted at the sight of her hijab tilted to the side. Taking a pin, she tied the cloth under her chin.

This was not the way her mum had taught her. She knew it would irritate her mum for what she was sure would be a ridiculous reason, but it was the easiest way she had found; shown to her by one of her best friends at school.

She chuckled at the thought of that friend. Her name was Zaynab, and she was already married with a child on the way. An arranged marriage. And here she was, at university, dating a man from a separate culture – just waiting for the aftermath from her own disapproving family.

How times change.

Finally, she fixed the last piece of her hijab around the back of her head in a loop, bringing the shorter side around her front, allowing it to spill down her chest.

She looked herself in the eyes.

Some people in this world would try to make her hate herself for what she was. She didn't even know how many people, in fact, until she undertook this assignment.

Giving herself a final deep look in her eyes, she vowed to herself never to let those people succeed.

She was proud of who she was.

She was proud of her background.

That would never change.

With a final flicker of a smile, she grabbed her keys and left the room.

CHAPTER TWO

Eric's brain ached.

He was starting to find books infuriating and tedious. Which was ridiculous. He had grown up with books. All he ever did as a teenager was curl up on the sofa and read.

He chose to study English Literature as his undergraduate for a reason; books were his escape. For the introvert, books are often the only way to escape from the noisy, monotonous, ravenous jungle of the city life you come from. Eric was no exception to this.

It was just the books they were forcing him to read…

Wuthering Heights. Pride and Prejudice. Sign of the Four. All stunning, marvellous works of literature – in their time.

But boy, did Eric hate them.

He fell in love with fantasy, science fiction, horror. He admired the likes of Stephen King, Derek Landy, J. K. Rowling.

He couldn't care less whether Elizabeth Bennett got married.

Sauntering up to the bar of the student union whilst stifling a yawn, he glanced at the time. Midday.

Thank Christ for afternoon naps, he thought to himself – then recalled the plans he had made with Suniya.

Still, a day with Suniya is far better than sleep.

"Can I get a coffee, please? And a packet of salt and vinegar crisps," he requested from the barmaid, who shot him an irritable look. Eric assumed this was for ordering a coffee at the bar when the university has a sufficient coffee shop just around the corner.

But why would they serve coffees here if they didn't want you to buy them?

Shying away from the glare, he faced downwards to avoid having to make uncomfortable eye contact with her again.

He cast his mind back to Suniya, to more pleasant trails of thought.

Yes, that's the great thing about Suniya. We barely even think about sleep...

He grinned to himself. She was damn sexy, despite assumptions people may make when meeting her. Honestly, people not seeing the amazing, sensual woman she was upon first meeting her was something Eric relished; he didn't particularly encourage competition.

"Thank you," he said to the barmaid, ensuring to show an extra-large smile of gratitude for going to the lengths of making him a coffee; a token of appreciation responded to by the roll of her eyes.

He turned and immediately bumped into some bloke charging past.

"Sorry," Eric offered as the hot coffee spilt down his jeans, scalding his crotch. He stifled his irritable expression as the man glanced back, wanting to make sure he did not cause offense.

The man decided to ignore Eric, instead greeting his mates with a laddish, "Oi! Oi!"

Eric sat at the only free table in the student union bar,

tucking his bag underneath his chair to ensure he didn't make anyone fall over. He withdrew his Kindle and opened page eighty-nine of 'Return of the King'. He counted this as the eighth time he had read the Lord of the Rings trilogy – and it was still as enthralling as the first.

"All right, luv!" wailed a laddish bloke, taking the table adjacent to Eric's, along with three of his mates. An attractive woman walked past, tutting as they all leered at her.

"I'd love to show you my cock!" another one of the blokes jeered, causing rapturous laughter amongst his friends.

Eric shook his head in disbelief. How someone could shout such horrible things at an innocent woman minding her own business, he did not know.

As one of the blokes acknowledged Eric's irritable glare, he immediately flinched his head away and returned to his Kindle, hoping not to cause any hostility from his disdain.

After a few seconds, the chauvinistic group of lads returned to their midday pints of lager and laddish conversation, ignoring Eric. Eric let out a sign of relief, from a breath he hadn't realised he was holding.

"This fackin' bitch last night, mate," one of the blokes blurted out, speaking far louder than he needed to. Eric assumed this was to show off to anyone who could overhear them but, fearing a negative reaction, made sure not to show this private judgment on his face. "I couldn't believe her, mate; had a pussy the size of a bucket."

The rest of his mates cackled along.

Eddie stifled a flinch at the revolting remarks made, attempting to refocus his attention solely on what Frodo and Samwise were doing.

"Mate, you are such a dickhead."

"Fuck off, you should ah seen her tits, they were fuckin' huge."

"Wouldn't mind a go on those."

"Mate, I did have a fuckin' go on 'em an' all. Pulled it out all over 'em and she didn't even fuckin' stop me 'til it was covered over her fuckin' face."

"Bet it made her eye fuckin' shut an' all."

"Couldn't get it open!"

They all laughed with furious glee at the expense of this poor, wretched woman this man had likely abused the previous night.

If there had even been a woman at all.

"Mackin' on 'em hoes again mate, fuckin' sick!"

Just concentrate on your book. Ignore them, concentrate on your book. Then they won't bother you.

One of the lads glanced at Eric, who did his best to keep his gaze fixed on his Kindle. Despite not acknowledging any of the words he had read for at least two pages, he was desperate to give the impression that he was immersed in the latest chapter.

They aren't going to hurt you, Eric. Just leave them be.

The lad laughed oafishly at the sight of Eric, a timid man with glasses, gangly arms and scruffy hair, turning to his mates with a cocky smirk.

It's fine. Just ignore them and they'll leave you alone.

The lad nodded his head toward Eric and the rest of them stifled a laugh.

Please, just go. Leave them and go.

"Mate, this fuckin' geek is proper weird."

Without any hesitation, Eric shoved his Kindle into his bag. Leaving his coffee half-drunk, he slung his bag over his shoulder and marched out of the student union bar.

He heard the group of lads laughing behind him.

He told himself he was pathetic. Ridiculous. Couldn't even have a coffee without being intimidated.

He tried to convince himself they were not laughing at him. They were a bunch of sexist idiots, yes, but they weren't laughing at him.

Doesn't matter. Got to leave anyway. Got to meet Suniya.

Even though he wasn't meeting his girlfriend for another fifteen minutes, he still persuaded himself that was the reason for his departure. Nothing to do with those lads. It was entirely because he didn't want to be late. Even though it took him less than five minutes to get to his room.

Sure, Eric. Sure, that's why.

Doesn't matter.

Hate to be late.

That's why.

Totally the reason why. Lateness is irritating. Eric was never late.

He shook his head to himself.

You're pathetic.

Mentally scolding his pathetic, easily intimidated mind, he deliberately veered down a longer path so as not to have to ask two women in the midst of conversation to let him pass.

CHAPTER THREE

Flashing his cheekiest grin at his beastly reflection, Bruno Tug smoothed down his suit jacket. He grazed his hand over his closely shaven skinhead, and his eyes flickered with smugness at the new tattoo on his neck.

A Celtic cross, gloriously displayed next to his England flag.

With a final, sneaky glance, he straightened his tie and fastened his top button.

Shooting himself another sneer at his intimidatingly alpha appearance, he grabbed his phone from the side of his bed, opened the news app and cackled triumphantly.

English Hearts announce protest in Stoke-on-Trent.

Tucking his phone into his pocket, he leisurely strolled downstairs and into the kitchen.

His wife had already placed his coffee on the table and was preparing his toast. His two daughters sat obediently eating their cereals.

Bruno beamed as he marvelled at his kingdom. He meandered to his wife, placing a kiss on her cheek and making her giggle as she grazed his stubble. As she turned and tittered, he retracted his arm and landed an outstretched paw against her backside, grabbing her arse cheeks fully in his hands, causing her to jump and snigger.

"All right darlin'?" he greeted her, his voice rough and coarse, displaying the working class roots he was so very proud of.

"All right my lovely!" replied Sharnelle, her smile like sunshine between curls of her straight, blond hair. "Breakfast won't be a min. 'Ave a seat, babe."

Bruno pulled out a chair and sat at the end of the table, gazing proudly upon his two daughters.

"Don't I got no kisses for Daddy?" he prompted.

With eager, loving acceleration, both daughters jumped out of their seats and planted a kiss on his bristly cheek before returning to their respective breakfasts.

"Soya, what you got at school today?" Bruno asked his eldest daughter. Twelve years old and an incredibly smart girl, she was already top of her class in everything.

"Well, Daddy," she began, "I have maths first with Miss Smith, English with Mr. Holdsworth, then Science, then Geography, then Drama."

Bruno smirked. She loved drama. So self-confident and assured, she was a brilliant performer.

As Sharnelle leant over Bruno's shoulder to place his breakfast in front of him, he took a moment to admire his wife. Slim, with a prominent, large chest; his dream woman.

"What about you, my sweet?" Bruno directed at his youngest daughter.

"Today," replied seven-year-old Stacey, her pretty face smiling enthusiastically under her light-blonde hair, "I have Science all morning, then we have Religious Studies with Mrs. Patel."

"Who?" barked Bruno.

"With Mrs. Patel, Daddy."

Bruno's eyes narrowed. His smile faded, replaced by an ominous, grim façade his family had grown to know all too well.

"What is she, Mrs. Patel? A bloody paki, or what?"

"I think so, Daddy," sang out Stacey innocently.

"Then don't you listen to a fuckin' word of it, my sweet." Bruno wagged his thick, sausage-like finger. "You go along with it, like, do the work an' all that, don't get in no trouble or nothin'. Just don't forget what she is, yeah?"

"What is she, Daddy?" Stacey asked, her sweet, innocent, wide eyes peering up at her hero.

"She is no good, Islamic, immigrant scum," he told her, slowly and specifically, ensuring to pronounce each and every syllable.

"Okay, Daddy," smiled Stacey, diving her spoon into her cereal and gathering as much onto it as she could.

"Good girl," Bruno proudly declared.

CHAPTER FOUR

Tapping lightly at the door, Suniya felt a tingle of excitement.

She always had the same tingle run through her body when tapping on Eric's door. He was handsome, but intelligently so; Suniya had never been one for pretty boys, far preferring her man to have an air of social awkward cleverness to them. Eric was just that. Thin and gangly, and with glasses perched astutely on his nose, he was the exact embodiment of the person you would want to take home to meet your mum.

Except, the idea of him meeting Suniya's family wasn't making her so excited. Willing herself to bury such trepidation to the back of her mind, she flung her arms around his neck and embraced him with a long, passionate, enthused kiss.

"Hey," she smiled sweetly at him, not removing her arms from around his neck.

"Hey yourself," he replied, his arms tucked neatly around her waist.

Without a moment's hesitation, he kicked the door closed, picked her up with a struggle Suniya ignored and laid her on the bed.

He kissed her once more, running his hand down the side of her face and down her perfectly curved body.

"How were lectures?" Suniya asked between kisses, peering seductively into his eyes.

"Wonderful," Eric lied. "And you?"

"Ah, no lecture today. But a riveting assignment about the psychology of racial prejudices."

"Sounds entrancing."

"Really was. You should read it."

"Sure. But I'd rather do this."

He sank his lips into hers, enjoying the subtle scent of her perfume. He tucked his hand up her dress, rubbing along her smooth legs and up her waist.

"Not now, you naughty boy!" Suniya joked. "We have places to be."

Eric smiled and obediently removed his hand.

"Are you nervous?" she pondered.

"I don't know. Should I be?"

Suniya hesitated.

Sensing a deep conversation approaching, Eric flumped from his mounting position and onto his side, indenting himself in the bed next to her. She turned toward him and they tucked their arms around each other, laying on the pillow of his single bed, happily forced up against each other.

"Have you ever met any parents before?" she asked, not sure whether she really wanted the answer.

"I haven't really had any parents to meet, to be honest."

It was true. Both of them were relatively inexperienced when it came to relationships. Whilst she was growing up her family had been strict, and there had never been an opportunity for her to bring a guy home. For Eric, it wasn't that he was not allowed; more that girls had never paid him much attention.

It wasn't until they met on fresher's night out eight months ago that he had finally mustered the courage to speak to a girl.

Though if he was honest, she was the one who spoke to him first.

"Do you think it matters?" Eric started, not sure how to approach the question he wished to ask. "Do you think it'll bother them that I'm, you know... white?"

"White? No." Suniya shook her head. "Not Muslim? Yes," she added, before he could breathe any sigh of relief.

"What do you think they might do?"

"I have no idea. Kick me out the house. Disown me. Chase you down the street."

"Are you being serious?"

Suniya thought for a moment. "I'm not sure," she laughed.

Eric sighed.

"Maybe this isn't a good idea," he suggested.

"Maybe not, but what are we going to do? Keep you a secret forever? They need to meet you, Eric."

"Do they know I'm not Muslim?"

"I told my sister. I don't know if she told my parents."

Eric rolled his eyes back and lifted his head in exasperation, rendered severely anxious.

"Eric, look at me," she demanded, lifting a hand to the side of his face and forcing his worried gaze to meet hers. "It doesn't matter. Honestly. It's not going to change a single thing about how much I love you."

"Really?"

"Promise. I mean, would it bother you if your family didn't like me?"

Eric laughed. "To be honest, I think they'd just be grateful I actually have a girlfriend."

She smiled and rested her forehead gently on his.

"I love you," she asserted, her face growing serious.

"I love you, too."

They engaged in a short, tender kiss.

Eric friskily lifted an eyebrow.

"Sure we haven't got, I don't know… ten minutes?"

Suniya checked the clock behind her.

"We haven't really…" she began, then paused mid-thought, turning back to Eric with a wicked smirk. "Oh, screw it. We'll be ten minutes late."

Their lips met, their hands instantly moving all over each other.

They left an hour later.

CHAPTER FIVE

FOR NINETEEN YEARS, it had been the same old story.

Get out of bed. Put on your uniform, fasten your belt, tip your hat. Kiss Vanessa goodbye, promise her you'll be safe. Go to work, aware that she worries about you every damn minute. As does your mother. And anyone else who cares about you.

And, if he was honest with himself, Jack Taylor would have to admit that being a policeman had left him jaded. He was accustomed to the rash and ill-timed jokes his colleagues made at the sight of dead bodies, jokes that he was so appalled about when he began at the age of nineteen.

Just the previous day, they came across a man who had hung himself from a lamp-post. As one of the other officers left, he had retorted, "Well, best not hang around."

It wasn't even just that Jack found himself laughing at such comments. It was that they didn't affect him anymore.

That's what really made him decide he'd been on the beat for too long. Not the fact that he had become immune to the sight of blood, dead children, or foul language spewing from the mouth of a drunk; it was once he had become immune to the disgusting jokes. Like poorly timed offensive comments didn't matter anymore.

It had all changed two years ago.

On the day Tallah was born.

Having a daughter changes you. Now, when Jack sees that dead child, he worries that it could someday be his baby child. When he sees blood, it could be his daughter's. When a drunk shouts abuse, it could one day be at her expense.

And when an officer makes jokes about an innocent person who had committed suicide by hanging themselves from a lamp-post... What if, heaven forbid, someday that was his daughter they were making the joke about?

He never said any of this, of course. He didn't want his wife to worry. She was his childhood sweetheart and, inevitably, knowing her for so many years meant that he knew her very well.

He knew she worried. He knew she spent all day thinking terrible, anxious thoughts. The unconscious mind of a worrier is that person's worst enemy. It will inflict thoughts, comments, and images upon you that you can never find a way to control.

So, just as he would any other day, Jack pulled on his shirt, his black tie, his stab-proof vest, his hat, and his high-vis jacket that read POLICE in capital letters on its back; the jacket that made everyone stare at him wherever he went.

Then, finally, he placed his jacket under his arm as he fastened his belt, laden with handcuffs, CS spray, and an asp.

He scoffed. An asp.

What would an asp do against a psychopath with a gun?

It was like a thick stick that police ran around with. What are you supposed to do when you face someone with a real weapon?

Not that he had ever faced a person with a gun, but the thought still amused him. A niggling thought in the back of his mind. A frequent reminder that it only takes one person to be carrying such a weapon for its use to be fatal at his expense.

As he left the bedroom, he could hear his wife clinking around in the kitchen downstairs. He took the descent of the stairs steadily, savouring each moment it took to approach her. More than two decades together, and he still loved her more and more each day.

"Hey," he announced himself, kissing his wife on the cheek.

"Hey to you, too," Vanessa replied, responding with a deep, meaningful kiss. "How are you feeling after yesterday?"

Jack had forgotten about that.

He had made the mistake of telling Vanessa how he was tired of the endless spewing of racial abuse he received as a police officer. Given, not too long ago, even being a black police officer would have been an incredible accomplishment. Now, he had the same opportunities to rise the ranks as all the other constables.

But the people he arrested didn't feel the same.

And he would not be able to go longer than a week without hearing someone say, "Fuck off darky," or, "What do you know? You're just a nigger."

He was in charge of a unit tackling violent racism, so it was something he knew he had to get used to. And he had. It was just... more recently, it had started to grate on him.

He had confided in Vanessa that he believed it was becoming a father that had made him more susceptible to dark thoughts.

"Yeah, I'll be fine," he assured her, forcing a smile. "I've heard it all before."

"Yeah, I know. But I worry about you."

"Well, you needn't," he told her, kissing her delicately on the forehead.

Then he turned toward the miracle that sat at the kitchen

table in her high chair, beaming a sweet, adorable smile up at her father.

"How are you doing?" Jack enthusiastically asked his daughter.

"Hi, Daddy!" Tallah sang out, her beautiful voice a luxury to his ears.

Every day she made him proud, just by smiling her cheerful, cheeky grin at him.

Ten years she had taken to conceive.

Ten long, hard, strenuous years.

They thought it was never going to happen.

Yet, there she was, sat happily in the kitchen, gleefully unaware that her breakfast was all over her face.

As he braced himself to leave, shoving two bananas into his bag and taking his coffee flask off his wife, he took a moment to look at his family.

Long, dark hair framed Vanessa's delicate face. She had the same sass as his mother, and it was one of the things he loved most about her. More and more, he could pick up on Tallah echoing that sass, with her cheeky grin and naughty giggles.

"I love you," he told his wife.

"I love you too," she answered with a kiss.

He gave his daughter a kiss on the forehead, telling her he loved her also.

"Love you too, Daddy!" she grinned.

And, with that, he left.

For the longest day at work he would ever have.

CHAPTER SIX

It was perfect.

Absolutely fucking perfect.

Karl Jenkins had never made anything like it before.

He took a moment, leaning back in his chair, surveying the computer screen with gleeful, triumphant eyes.

What a beauty.

What an absolute bloody beauty.

It was nothing like he'd made before. Using years of expertise, months of work, and a lifetime of being a loser cast out of any social group that would have him.

Well, screw them.

Who was laughing now?

This virus was perfect. The malware was perfect. It would do the job and more.

The only regret was that he couldn't meet Bruno Tug to show him the product himself. That would be a dream. To actually meet him. Every time he spoke to the guy on the phone, he got butterflies in the belly.

Some people saw him as a legend. An idol. An icon for the righteous movement of the modern age.

Karl didn't see him like that.

Bruno was oh so much more.

He was a messiah. The second coming. A revolutionary.

The guy would go down in history as the great man, greater than anyone who had come before him, the one who destroy Muslim fascism once and for all.

And his ability to do that would be all down to Karl.

Karl, who had kept his ability to hack expertly secret from the world, until now – for this very purpose.

Because once he had hacked into every power company operating the city of Stoke-on-Trent and released his malware, there would be nothing those helpless, clueless idiots could do.

And when he used the government database to track the GPS of every phone number located in the city of Stoke-on-Trent, that agency wouldn't even know it was him until the virus had hit.

And that virus.

Oh, that sweet, sweet virus.

The first virus to be delivered to mobile phones on a mass basis, ever. The digital age was still so fresh, so new, that no one quite understood how someone like Karl could use his abilities to do such a thing,

But soon they would.

He was going to singlehandedly shut down the city of Stoke-on-Trent.

And Bruno would be so proud.

Oh so, so proud.

Especially when Karl ensured there was no way they would be able to get the information out of him as to how to reverse it.

The city would be plunged into darkness. No way they can communicate with the outside.

And then the English Hearts would cleanse it.

They will make this country right again, starting with this city.

He was so excited.

He could feel it in his bones.

The time was near.

They all underestimated him. They all called him a loser, ignored him, told him he would never amount to anything.

Fucking idiots don't have a clue what is coming.

STAFFORDSHIRE ONLINE
ENGLISH HEARTS ARRIVE IN STOKE-ON-TRENT

The infamous, far-right protest movement English Hearts, arrives in Stoke-on-Trent today for their day of protesting against the rise of Islamism and apparent Sharia law in the United Kingdom.

Claiming that it will be a peaceful protest, we interviewed their leader, Bruno Tug.

"We are here for a peaceful protest," he told us. "But we will not tolerate anti-free speech groups that get in our way. It is our right to let our opinion be known. We are a human rights organisation, and we are here to fight for the rights in England, and Britain, to go to those that are English and British."

Describing himself as a radical patriot, Tug continues to object to those who say his group is racist. Instead, he says that they harbour the belief that the religion of Islam challenges the English Christian way of life.

The group's previous leader, Jason Harbridge, left the group after Bruno Tug took over, claiming that the group's intentions had gone beyond that of a street protest, citing dangers of the group being led to far-right extremism. These are accusations that Tug furiously denies.

Whatever you think of the group, their past association with violence has undeniably left many in counter-protests wounded. Tug continues to say, however, that these people do not represent the true members of the English Hearts.

"We have the right, having been born in this country, to fight for the *right of those who belong to this country. We need to make these people know that their ideologies are not welcome here. We are a Christian country, and we will stay with these roots, and we will not let them get corrupted by a religious group that incites fear in the West."*

Tug appears passionate about what he's saying, first seen in his initial rise to fame when he featured in a video that leaked online and went viral. In it, he said, "Muslims worship a prophet who was a paedo; I mean, he shagged a nine-year-old, didn't he?"

With this being the first protest under Tug's reign, we are still yet to see the direction this group will go in. Nevertheless, Stoke-on-Trent will be home to their protest, peaceful or not.

CHAPTER SEVEN

Eric felt Suniya's wary gaze. His anxiety was stamped all over his face. The various cautious glances she kept throwing his way were only making it worse. Knowing she was looking, he willed himself to control it, but it was no good. His brow perspired and his arms were even shaking.

Eric wished he could reassure Suniya that he was fine. But all he could do was keep playing through all the awful ways this day could pan out, as if each scenario was projected onto a cinema screen in his mind.

Nightmare Scenario One. Suniya's father gets so appalled at the sight of a white non-Muslim approaching the house, holding his daughter's hand, he takes out a gun and chases Eric not only down the street, but for a solid hour through Birmingham City Centre.

Which was bizarre, he knew. It was incredibly unlikely that a well-mannered family in the UK would be hiding a stash of guns.

So maybe I can rule that scenario out.

Nightmare Scenario Two. Her father brings out that dagger

that they carry around for their religion and chases him with that.

But wait.

Oh shit. Muslims don't carry that. That's Sikhs I'm thinking of. And it's called a kirpan. I'm so bad. I'm so, so bad. I don't even know about the religion of the woman I love. How bad am I?

Nightmare Scenario Three. Her father picks up on how little he actually knows about the Islamic faith and, as a test of whether Eric is to be approved or not, Suniya's father forces him to take a written exam on the Muslim religion. An exam that he fails terribly.

But at least I know how little I know. I'm not pretending not to. I mean, surely that will count in my favour.

He considered this for a few moments, then decided it was unlikely.

If I don't even know the minute details of Suniya's religion, how on earth would he think I'm worthy of dating her?

The thing is, Suniya's religion had never been a problem to Eric. Nor to Suniya, as far as he was aware. They'd had a brief conversation at the start of their relationship where they had shared what they believed, but that was just to get it all out in the open. They had never needed to discuss their beliefs because, well, they had never been an issue.

Until now.

Nightmare Scenario Four. *They kill me.*

He chuckled at himself, marvelling at the audacity of his ridiculous thoughts.

"What is it?" Suniya asked, seeing the knowing smile on his face.

"Nothing," Eric replied. "I'm just thinking about all the ways today could go wrong."

Suniya gave a sympathetic smile and squeezed his hand, a gesture Eric had come to appreciate. He was frequently nervous and frequently overthinking, and the squeeze of his hand was a gesture Suniya always used to reassure him.

Strange, really. How the simple act of a small amount of applied pressure on his hand could completely change his emotional state.

She reassured him that whatever happened, she was going nowhere.

Isn't that all that matters?

A bus came to a halt at the bus stop.

Their transport to the train station had arrived. All those nerves Eric had just managed to quell immediately resurfaced. This was their chariot of fire to deliver them to the flames.

Suniya stepped onto the bus and gave the driver her money. Eric followed, producing a five-pound note.

"Nah, we don't take notes," declared the bus driver.

"Well, I don't have anything less," Eric shrugged, caught like a deer in the headlights.

"Don't matter, don't take notes."

"The fiver won't have much change."

"Don't matter, don't take 'em."

"Fine, just don't give me change."

"Can't do that. Not allowed. Against policy, innit?"

Eric was frozen to the spot. Panicking. How on earth were they going to make the train on time if he wasn't allowed on the damn bus?

Suniya appeared at his side with a handful of change.

"Here." She glared at the bus driver, who consequently nodded Eric onto the bus.

They took a seat on the third row from the front, as they had gotten used to. Eric liked to avoid the first two rows, as they were dedicated to the old and the disabled, but he also liked to avoid the back of the bus as well. He would tell Suniya this was because he became travel sick, which was true; but the truth was that he grew easily intimidated by the young, rowdy yobs that tended to aim for the back of the bus.

He'd recently had to sit toward the back during rush hour when there was no other space. A group of teenage lads had played a racket of loud, electronic music on their phones, talking in a vulgar manner about "dicks" and "pussies." Eric hadn't the guts to tell them to turn the music off or curb their language and instead had sat with his arms shaking, desperately willing the bus to hurry up.

He'd even gotten off the bus two stops too early and walked.

As Suniya and Eric waited for the bus to leave, the last two passengers got on. They were two lads, likely in their early twenties, joking and being loud.

"You're a fuckin' mong, mate," one of them laughed. "Can't believe you fuckin' did that!"

"She was pinin' for it, bruv!" exclaimed the other.

One of them paid with a five-pound note and they took a seat behind Suniya and Eric.

Eric closed his eyes, bowing his head in frustration.

Why? Why do they have to sit behind us? There is a whole bus void of people, why behind us?

He could feel Suniya's lingering stare. She gazed at him, a face full of confused concern.

"Are you all right?" she asked, putting her hand on his leg.

"Yeah, fine," he replied, knowing she was trying to figure out what was making him so shifty – the looming visit to her parents, or the two rowdy lads behind.

In truth, he had forgotten all about the visit to her parents.

"It's okay," she reassured him, affectionately stroking his leg. "It's fine."

He bowed his head and sighed, closing his eyes for a brief moment, willing himself to stop being such a coward.

As the bus drove away and took them on their journey, he managed to direct his thoughts elsewhere. Becoming secure in the belief that the two lads were not going to interfere with them, he managed to tune out their loud, boisterous conversation and distract himself with other thoughts.

He considered his latest university assignment. It required him to study a book of the classic literary genre; not a genre Eric particularly enjoyed. He despised classic literature; he loved more modern, exciting books that would take him away to various worlds, from epic fantasy to time-travel science fiction.

Out of the corner of his eye, he caught a glimpse of something distracting him.

One of the lads behind him.

He was stroking his hand down Suniya's hijab.

Suniya was currently unaware, but Eric could see them, the mocking stroke of a hand running itself down a piece of trailing cloth.

The two lads sniggered.

Eric kept his eyes focused forward. He kept tunnel vision, dead set before him, focussing on where the bus was going.

If he didn't see it, he wouldn't be expected to do or say anything.

Hopefully, they would stop, and Suniya would be able to go about the rest of the day unaware.

Hopefully.

Suniya's head yanked backward in a slight jerk. She scowled and looked over her shoulder.

"Sorry, love," one of the blokes grunted, grinning at her, and she turned her head away.

The two men stifled a giggle.

She looked at Eric, to see if he had noticed.

Eric had. But he was not looking at her.

He was looking dead ahead.

Fixedly staring at the road.

Didn't see it. Don't need to do anything. Don't need to say anything.

Please don't do it again. Please, please, please.

Suniya sighed and looked out the window. Eric could sense her frustration, but knew it would pass within a few minutes.

Her head jerked back once more, this time in a bigger, more violent motion.

"Can you stop it?" Suniya barked, snapping her head around.

"Sorry, love, my mistake again," the bloke smirked.

"I know what you're doing," Suniya assertively exclaimed, not backing down. "Can you knock it off?"

Please don't wind them up, Suniya. Please. It will be me they attack, not you. Please don't wind them up.

Suniya turned her head back around and shot another look at Eric.

Eric did not return the gaze. He could feel her held stare, firing daggers at his face, but he did not look back.

The bus turned a corner.

The train station was near.

Just a few more minutes.

Just don't do anything stupid, Suniya, please.

"What is your problem?" Suniya stood up and shouted.

Eric hadn't even noticed they had done it again. He was so focussed ahead of himself, so adamant in tuning it out, that he hadn't noticed the big grab of her hijab in the greasy fist of the irritating lad behind.

The two men didn't say anything to Suniya. Instead, they got up and left the bus as it pulled up to their stop, in absolute hysterics. They were practically falling over each other they were cackling so hard.

Once they had left, the bus drove away and Suniya retook her seat. She turned to Eric, shooting him a menacing glare.

"Did you not see that?" she demanded.

"I–" he stuttered, not knowing what to say. "I thought it was best to just ignore them."

Suniya didn't give him a verbal response. She didn't need to. The angry purse of her lips pressed tightly together said it all. She folded her arms, shook her head, and crossed her legs away from him.

He attempted to put his hand in hers.

She let him.

But she didn't grasp back. Nor did she squeeze, or move her hand from her folded arms.

Eric willed her not to be mad. He willed her to think he did the right thing.

"They were arseholes," Eric weakly offered.

"Yeah," replied Suniya forcefully, staring out the window. "They were."

If I'd have said something, it would have just become a confrontation. I did the right thing in ignoring it.

That was what he kept telling himself.

Over and over again, he willed himself to believe that he did the right thing.

He knew it was a lie.

He knew he was just trying to convince himself.

But if he kept saying it, maybe it would be true. Maybe she would forgive him and see that he was just trying to avoid a fight.

He bowed his head and retracted his hand.

No. I didn't do nothing because I thought it was right. I did nothing because I'm scared.

They spent the rest of the journey to the train station in silence.

CHAPTER EIGHT

It was such a lovely day. It was the kind of day you spend ages hoping for, only to decide that it is too hot. The sun beamed overhead, people leisurely walked around in joyous moods, adorned in their shorts and t-shirts, finally set free from the confines of their cupboards.

But for Jack, the weather wasn't relevant. He still wore the same dark-blue tunic, stab-proof vest, and a hard helmet. It made him sweat, but it kept him safe – and he felt proud to wear it.

Especially now. He and his team's nine-month investigation that had been incredibly successful in tracking some of Britain's most extreme British racist groups was nearing its end. Forty persistent offenders had been arrested and charged. That meant there were forty fewer scumbags spreading their racial hatred across the streets of the United Kingdom.

His wife and daughter were a little bit more safe.

But there was one final target.

And now it was time to hand that target, and their intelligence, over to the Chief Inspector for the final part of the plan – nailing Bruno Tug.

The leader of the English Hearts.

There had been nothing concrete they could use against Tug, so had been unable to convict him of the horrific attitudes he had expressed. He was a man who was so blatantly racist, but never allowed himself to openly do anything he could be charged for – and it had been immensely frustrating.

And now he was leading the English Hearts. And Jack would follow Bruno Tug throughout this protest, trail him wherever he would go, hoping for something to use. Hoping he could witness one of the horrendous acts Tug committed.

Jack stopped his car beside an off-license and stepped out, squinting in the morning sunshine. As he entered the shop, he noticed a gang of youths hanging around on bikes on the corner of the road. Burberry caps, tracksuit bottoms, glaring cockily at the sight of his uniform.

After lingering his gaze on these boys for a few fleeting seconds, he recognised one of them as a lad called Billy. Billy was a well-known local racist who had been oddly quiet lately.

In fact, they had all been oddly quiet lately.

Jack put it down to the success of his operation that racism in the area was lessening. But it just seemed off. Which was odd to admit, but it was true; it was unsettling. As if there was something they were missing.

He ignored what he thought were a few "oinks" muttered in his direction by the lads. He could confront them, but what was the point? He had a big day and didn't need the fuss.

He looked over the options in the fridge and settled for a Diet Coke and a Boost bar. He paid for his things, nodded at the shop owner, and made his way to his car.

As he placed his drink and snack on the car roof, fumbling for his keys, that's when he heard it.

"All right piggy," came a low-pitched, subtly quiet tease from the group of lads behind him.

Just ignore it. You've got a big day and you don't want to waste your time.

Jack opened the car door, threw his items on the passenger seat, and went to climb in.

"All right nigger."

He froze.

He couldn't ignore that. There was no way he was ignoring that.

With an exasperated huff, he climbed out of the car and meandered over to the lads on the bikes. They smirked at him like cocky hyenas, leering and grinning with triumphant glee.

Jack knew he shouldn't have gone over. He'd given them exactly what they wanted.

"Is there a problem, lads?" Jack asked, making sure to assume a strong, confident posture.

"No, Officer," one of them sang playfully, smirking at his mates.

"What about you, Billy?" Jack prompted, turning his head to the scrawniest one of the group.

"What problem would I have?" Billy asked, putting his arms out wide, looking around himself with a cocky front. "Sun's in the sky, birds are singing. It's a proper nice day to be alive, innit?"

Jack narrowed his eyes, trying to figure out what they were up to. He hated this arrogant strut and conceited attitude these kids were giving him. It was nothing he could particularly pick out, but they were deliberately pushing him, acting tough without directly saying anything of offense.

Jack hated it when they did that. How are you supposed to quote on a report, "they said it was a lovely day, which was offensive."

It's just something in the way they said it. The way they stood. The way their overbearingly smug faces leered at him with mocking pleasure.

"You getting smart with me?" Jack enquired.

"Can't I just enjoy the day?" Billy replied.

Deciding he'd had enough, Jack turned and walked back to the car.

And as he did, he swore he could hear one final comment being muttered at him, following by concealed chuckles of boastful laughter.

"Nigger."

CHAPTER NINE

THE TRAIN TO Stoke-on-Trent was a long, but satisfying, journey. Three hours from London, with one change at Birmingham New Street, then straight on through to sunny old Staffordshire.

Bruno had visited Stoke-on-Trent once before for a day's training when he had started working at the tyre outlet, back before he ran the business. Even then, he had found himself traipsing heavily through Hanley town centre, disgusted at what surrounded him.

Everywhere he looked, they were there. It was like a 'Where's Wally?' – except Wally was all the British people.

The last time he had visited, the cricket was on – India against Great Britain.

India had won.

Traffic had been forced to halt. He had sat idly in his car, getting increasingly infuriated, as the Indian population of Stoke-on-Trent took to the street to celebrate.

Indian men cloaked in Indian flags, cheering and chanting in some foreign language; Bruno couldn't understand who they thought they were, parading down a street they had no right to parade down.

It was disgusting.

That was why he had chosen Stoke-on-Trent.

This town would not know what hit them.

As the train filled up, Bruno noticed there were no longer any seats vacant. A heavily pregnant woman clambered onto the train, hobbling on after everyone else, struggling to keep going as her hands clutched onto her belly.

Not a soul helped her.

"'Scuse me, love," Bruno offered. "Would you like my seat?"

"Oh, really?" replied the pregnant woman. "That is so kind."

"Think nothin' of it, darlin', 'ere you are."

Bruno stood up, addressing the woman with a large, welcoming smile, and took to standing in the centre aisle with the few stragglers who hadn't made it on in time to claim a seat.

Figuring it would be an opportune time to confirm a few of the arrangements for the day's events, he whipped out his phone. As he lit the screen, he saw he already had several messages. He opened them, starting with the first:

Bruno mate, our gas supply might be getting stopped. No gas, no fire.

Bruno let out an exasperated sigh. Must he do everything himself?

Speak to the copper called Roland. He will sort you out.

After no more than thirty seconds, he got a reply.

Spoken to Roland. We are en route with gas. Jake has the molotovs, all sorted his end.

He opened another message.

It's Karl. Say the words and the virus will be deployed.

Bruno pumped the air with a small fist – slyly, so as not to attract attention to himself.

Everything was going to plan.

It was going to be a magnificent day.

Feeling a stare, Bruno lifted his head and saw a brown-skinned fellow a few seats across the train, gormlessly staring at him. On his lap was a young, brown-skinned child.

"What the fuck you lookin' at?" Bruno barked.

The man abruptly flinched his gaze away and directed his eyes out the window.

Bruno did not. Long after the guy's eyes had been directed elsewhere, Bruno's glare was still fixed on him. And on the guy's son, who was still staring at him.

"You better stop your fuckin' kid starin' at me," Bruno demanded in a slow, quiet, seething voice that sent shivers through the man's spine.

"Come on Ahmed." The man spoke in a thick Indian accent, taking his son by the hand and leading him away.

Bruno watched until the man disappeared into the subsequent carriage, and took his seat.

His mouth moulded into a triumphant grin.

He lifted his phone once more as he received another message.

Everyone's gathering at two. Most are here already. Mate, they are well excited to meet you. It's gonna be amazing.

Bruno grinned.

A surge of pride soared through his body. It really was going to be amazing.

What an incredible achievement.

To have been able to organise what he had organised. To keep it concealed from the authorities if they indeed had managed to, was also a confounding victory.

If this worked...

If everything came off, everyone did what they needed to at the right time, if they were in the right positions...

They had many ex-military on their side. Soldiers who had served in Iraq and Afghanistan, who were sick of seeing the people they were killing taking over our own country, had eagerly joined them. And their input had been invaluable.

Their military expertise, not just on teaching everyone how to use the weapons, but in organising the sporadic attacks, coordinated at exact times for maximum impact, would be tremendous.

He saw a page from the newspaper a man across from him was reading.

It read that the English Hearts were visiting Stoke-on-Trent for a peaceful protest.

He couldn't help but laugh.

There was going to be nothing peaceful about it.

CHAPTER TEN

THE SHINING sun felt at odds with the darkness of the day's events. It was warm, and most officers gathered in the meeting room were in short sleeves. There was a buzz in the room, officers in high spirits, eager to make a difference.

For Jack, this was a proud moment. He had led the team here, now it was time to see all that work put into the final plan of action.

He sat at the back, where he could remain invisible. He ignored the common chatter and idle conversations, preferring to stay unnoticed than having to discuss the lovely weather in another meaningless conversation.

Eventually, Chief Inspector Lance Davis commanded a general shush as he took the front of the room. All eyes fell upon his confident demeanour. He was a bulky man, made of muscle you could only get if you spent an exorbitant amount of time in the gym – something Jack envied. He had spent much of his twenties lifting weights and he tried to avoid bad food; but when you get older, life tends to get in the way.

"Thank you, ladies and gentlemen, we will get started," began Davis, his shiny black goatee and slicked-back hair glistening in the window's spill of the sun. "As you all know, today is the protest of the English Hearts in Stoke-on-Trent. We have been lucky as Staffordshire police not to have to deal with too many far-right protests, and have managed to curb the ones we have dealt with fairly successfully. That being said, the group have a new leader, Bruno Tug, and the impression we get is that this man means business."

Davis clicked a mouse next to him and an image projected on the screen.

"This is Bruno Tug."

Jack smirked ironically at the man's skinhead and oafish exterior – Bruno was as Jack imagined your typical English Heart protestor to look. Call him cynical, but the skinhead in an anti-Islamic group suggested violence.

"Bruno Tug is a business-man, owning a tyre sales outlet in the East End of London. His criminal record is limited only to altercations with those of Indian, Pakistani, Polish, and African origin. He has been arrested for assault numerous times but has never been charged, and we have struggled to pin down anything we can get a conviction for. Still, he has a vicious online presence where he has launched scathing attacks at minorities. Have no qualms about it, officers – this man is a vicious racist, and he has violence in him."

Jack glanced at his watch. These briefings were all the same. He wanted to be out on the street facing this prick.

"They claim the protest to be a peaceful protest, and those who wish to protest peacefully will be allowed to do so. However, we will have riot gear police on standby in trucks that Sergeant O'Neil has organised at various points, and he will coordinate with those in the riot squad shortly after I have finished.

"They will start their protest in Stoke town centre, will make their way past the train station and the university, and into Hanley town centre. It is there that we expect any trouble that will occur to happen – as this is where the anti-English Hearts group are setting up their counter-protests.

"The first sign of disturbing the peace, and we need to be in there. Do not let anything get out of hand before we intervene. And, expect violence. Are there any questions?"

Blank faces stared back at CI Lance Davis.

"Right, let's get going."

All the officers were up at once, scuffling toward the door, getting ready for action.

Lance noticed how Jack was the last to go.

"How are you doing, Jack?" Lance asked.

"Brilliant, Inspector," Jack replied, a beaming smile and a buzzing body, poised on his heels with an eagerness to get started. "Just can't wait to finally nail this bastard."

CHAPTER ELEVEN

After a long, silent train ride, Suniya decided she was being immature. Yes, she was mad at Eric, but the silent treatment was made for children and idiots.

Maybe he had done the right thing, after all.

Maybe if Eric had stepped in and said something, it would have meant that it escalated.

Besides, she didn't want to have any tension between them as he met her parents. It wouldn't help the situation; the lunch was going to be stressful enough as it was.

The taxi pulled up outside her family home.

They were there.

Feelings of terror and trepidation overcame her. Then she realised that however anxious she was, it wouldn't be a touch on Eric's nerves.

She took his hand in hers and squeezed it.

"Just think, it's only a lunch, and later we have a lovely evening planned having drinks with Beth and Max," she comforted him, reminding him of their plans. "We just have to get through one meal, then we are out of here, and back to Stoke."

Eric nodded, staring at his feet.

"Okay," he whispered between frequent breaths. "Okay, let's do this."

"Eric." She turned his head toward her, cupping his worried face in her warm hands. "They are just people, okay? Whatever they think of you, I'll still love you, it won't change a thing. It will just take some getting used to, that's all."

He nodded, but his expression didn't change. The look of mortified hesitance remained.

Deciding they just needed to get in there and get the introductions over with, Suniya paid the driver, thanked him, then stepped out of the taxi. She took Eric's hand in hers, holding it tightly, as they edged down the garden path and toward the front door that was so familiar to Suniya, but so alien to Eric.

Placing three pronounced knocks on the door, she turned to Eric and looked him in the eyes.

"I'm going to let go of your hand now," she told him, keeping a soothing tone. "But that's because it might make my dad a bit nuts – but know that I still love you, and you're going to be fine."

She released her hand from Eric's relentlessly unwilling clutch just as the door swung open. A lady in her forties wearing a purple hijab held her arms open, ready to engulf Suniya.

"Suniya!" the woman ecstatically cried out, embracing her daughter. She wore numerous bracelets on her wrists that jangled as she swung her arms out. She struck Eric as quite tall and instantly loving toward her daughter.

"Mum, this is Eric, my boyfriend," she told her, holding her hand out to the terrified, nervous man rooted to the spot beside her. "Eric, this is my mum, Saida."

For a moment, Saida's gaze hung on Eric, stuck in a frozen second of perplexed undecidedness. She reminded Eric of his mum's cat who, when hearing an alien noise, would sit and stare at the source of that noise with a bemused expression as it tried to figure out what to make of it.

"Hello..." she eventually offered, breaking the uncomfortable silence, reluctantly releasing a hesitant hand for Eric to shake.

Eric took the hand and shook it until the brief greeting was over and Saida had swung back into the house.

Suniya raised her eyebrows at Eric and, with a whisper of, "You'll be okay," she entered, forcing him to follow.

As they entered the dining room, Eric marveled at the miraculously prepared dining table. Perfectly folded napkins sat next to precious, unmarked china. Wine glasses stood proudly around the graciously adorned table, accompanied by the smell of an inviting meal wafting in from the kitchen.

Suniya introduced her sister, Zakiyah, who was far more eager to meet him than her mum had been. Zakiyah was two years younger than Suniyah, but was still so confident and enthusiastic. Her subdued posture and pretty smile struck Eric, and he got the impression that she was a relaxed, open-minded woman, ready to face the mature world of adulthood. She flung her arms around Eric and keenly greeted him, making Eric feel a momentary tang of relief; at least someone here liked him.

Next was Suniya's aunt, whose reaction was even stronger than Saida's. She didn't even offer a hand to shake, or a smile to greet. Instead, she scrunched up her tiny, bird-like facial features, and recoiled in horror. She was a short, podgy lady covered in a baggy dress, with a plain brown hijab wrapped around her head.

"Kya ho raha hai!" Darya barked at her niece, Suniya.

"She doesn't speak a word of English," Suniya reassured him.

"Don't worry," smiled Zakiyah, standing comfortingly beside Eric. "It's probably best you don't understand what she's saying.

Zakiyah exchanged a knowing smile with Eric and, for a

brief moment, he felt grateful that he had someone on his side besides Suniya who would make him feel welcome.

Then her dad walked in.

Everyone fell silent, turning toward him with unanimously measured, worried stares. Precarious glances switched between them as the whole household fell to a deafening, awkward hush.

The tension rose, and Eric wished he could just turn around and run away.

Just do this for Suniya, he repeated to himself. *Just do this for Suniya. Just do this for Suniya.*

"This is my dad," Suniya cautiously introduced, carefully still, waiting to see what everyone would do next. "His name is Aabid."

"It's lovely to meet you," Eric announced.

Aabid didn't react. His authoritative, absent glare spoke volumes about his feelings. Eric prayed someone would say something, willed the family to break the unbearable coldness that had just consumed the room.

But no one did.

They all waited, eyes turned toward Aabid, to see how he would react.

"Dad, this is Eric," Suniya finally announced, urging Aabid to break the silence and show some kind of welcome to their guest.

Finally, Aabid twisted his cold stare away from Eric and to his hands, where the towel he had been using to dry them was poised.

"Let's eat," Aabid declared, and returned to the kitchen.

Eric let out a huge breath as soon as Aabid left the room.

Then he realised he would have to spend an entire meal with this man.

Suniya was at his side within seconds, placing a subtle, unnoticed hand gently on his back.

"Just relax," she assured him. "As soon as pudding's been eaten, we will go."

Suniya took her place at the table and prompted Eric to do the same with a demanding nod.

"Don't worry," Zakiyah mentioned to him as she took her place at the table. "It's just going to take a while. Maybe a long, long while."

Eric sat down cautiously. The whole time he was very aware that Darya was still staring at him with menacing eyes, whilst Saida was doing all she could to look the other way.

CHAPTER TWELVE

Bruno had endured very few moments as proud as this one.

The birth of his two daughters.

His wedding day.

Then this.

He took a satisfying moment, looking out over the sea of faces before him. He had never been more gratified, more honoured, or more privileged, to be surrounded by the people he had recruited.

And it was all because of him. All of this, every person there, every plan they had in place – it was down to him. He had done it. Sure, he'd had help from experts in their fields, but he had recruited them.

Now here were the 'peaceful protesters,' those with knowledge of his plans, ready to go out and make their voices heard.

Thousands of people filled the hall, filling it with delighted voices and excitable conversation. It was a tight squeeze, but no one objected. Each and every person wanted to be there and were ready for the fight ahead.

As Bruno took to the stage, he felt no nerves. Instead, he

felt a surge of adrenaline. An excited flutter in his belly, accompanied by an elated grin spread smugly across his face.

"Ladies and gentlemen!" he bellowed out, and every single member of the English Hearts protest for Stoke-on-Trent grew silent. "Welcome!"

Cheers and rapturous applause greeted his opening statement, filling him with venomous pride.

"Standing here today," he began, pacing the front of the stage, working the crowd, exuding his arrogant stage persona through his inherent presence. "Is the proudest moment I have had in my entire life."

More cheers. More applause. More enthusiastic shouts of support.

In his mind, Bruno likened himself to all the great speakers out there.

Franklin D. Roosevelt.

John F. Kennedy.

Winston Churchill.

And now him, Bruno Tug.

"As a child, my family had to scrimp and save. Because my dad was made redundant. He was thrown out on his arse, from a job he had built a career in for over twenty years. You know why?"

He gesticulated a grand point with his arm at the obedient crowd before him.

"Because Pakis came and stole it from him!"

Jeers rang around the spectators.

"His employer found an immigrant, who had forced his way into this, our brilliant country. And that immigrant was willing to do the job for less. So, my dad lost it! Meaning us, a patriotic, loving, working-class British family, were forced to live on scraps in a council estate in Woking!"

Screams of protestations, hollers of anger, and voices of detest filled the room.

"And what has changed in the last thirty years? I'll tell you what – not a fuckin' thing!"

Cheers of agreement appreciated what he declared.

"If anything, it's gotten worse! More and more I find this scum taking over *our* country. In the end, my father, the hardworking man I always looked up to as a child, ended up with fewer opportunities than the immigrants got. The *immigrant*, who came into *our* country, took *his* job. I ask you, was that right?"

"No!"

Bruno leant forward, lowering his voice, making the jeers and cheers quieten so they heard what he had to say.

"And were we allowed to say anything? Were we allowed to stand up and say, 'enough'? No! Because that would make us racist. Saying no to Muslims invading our country and our jobs meant that we were labelled as bad people.

"Well, today, I say no more.

"No more terrorists coming into this country. And that's what they are, terrorists – Muslims. The whole lot of them, Muslims.

"No more Sharia law laid down on our land.

"No more people telling us we can't stand up for the people who come from this country having the rights in this country. I'm sick of seeing off licenses, run by paki blokes who can't speak a word of fuckin' English, taking away business from supermarkets, with brands that are British institutions.

"Today it ends. We take back our country. Take it back from those brown fuckers who don't belong here. It's time to get passionate. It's time to get militant.

"*Are you with me?*"

Hands flung into the air in fists of agreement, accompanied by manic cheers of excited mutual views.

"This is a promise from me to you. English Hearts will no longer be some march that stands by and lets free speech reign against us. English Hearts will be a proud group of British people, with British genes, fighting for British rights."

Claps, applause, cheers.

"Pakis stole my dad's job. Pakis stole our country. Now Pakis will not take away our right to say enough!"

Bruno rose his hands into the air as the volume of his voice increased to meet the deafening agreement of his obedient audience.

"Because when we can't have the freedom to stand up to Islam's influence on British lives – that, my friends – is when liberty *dies*."

CHAPTER THIRTEEN

As Eric absentmindedly browsed the magazine shelf, his eyes fluttered between the alluring cover of *Empire* and the intriguing cover of *Sci-Fi Now*.

In truth, he'd been staring at them for almost five minutes, but could not recall what was on either of the covers. His mind dwelled on the awful lunch he had just endured.

He could honestly say it was probably the worst lunch he had ever endured.

Not the food – if anything, that was the lunch's redeeming feature. He'd had a wonderful jalfrezi with perfectly steamed rice that had almost scorched his mouth. But, not wanting to reveal to Suniya's family how useless he was with anything spicier than a korma, he had just resorted to numerous refills of water.

Now, there he was, reminiscing on what could accurately be recalled as a disaster. At Birmingham New Street Station. Waiting for Suniya to return from the toilet. Looking for a magazine to read on the train.

As Suniya approached, he decided against making a purchase. As much as he enjoyed reading a good feature on the latest exciting movie or fantasy novel, it would be a waste of money.

There was no way he was going to be able to focus on anything other than that meal.

"You ready to go?" prompted Suniya, with a forced smile.

Eric nodded and followed her out of the store. They found their way to their platform and boarded their train back to Stoke-on-Trent.

As they did, Eric couldn't help but notice a large number of people staring at them. Or, more accurately, at Suniya. Glares were etched over the faces of so many people travelling in, it made him feel both uncomfortable and wary.

Eric led them to the quiet coach, in hope that these people who kept staring would elect a coach that would give them freedom to be rowdy.

Eric lifted his head back and closed his eyes, letting out a long, exasperated sigh of relief. At least it was done. It was over.

He felt Suniya's hand in his, and he turned his gaze toward her. She had a sympathetic, forced smile that made it clear she knew just how he felt.

"My sister liked you," she offered.

Eric couldn't help but laugh. Suniya joined in, and together they had a good snigger at the ridiculousness of the situation. Once their laughing ended, they finally smiled at each other properly, having had the relief that they needed.

"Your sister was cool," Eric admitted. "I like her name, too. Zakiyah. It sounds, I don't know – exotic."

"Exotic?" Suniya raised her eyebrows and gave a chuckle at his expense. "Look, like I said, whatever happens, it doesn't change how I feel about you."

"Yeah, I know," Eric groaned, sighing once more. "I just... I really wanted them to like me. I wasn't expecting to be ignored for the entire lunch."

"I wasn't expecting that, either. Well, to be honest, I wasn't sure what I was expecting. But I knew it wouldn't be easy."

"I really tried."

Suniya cupped her hands around his face and turned him to look at her, being affectionately forceful, showing him with her eyes that she meant every word she said.

"It makes no difference. I know you tried, and that means the world to me. But they will like you. Just... not yet. Once they've gotten used to it."

She pulled his head forward and rested his forehead against hers. They both closed their eyes, sharing a moment of closeness before sealing their love with a long, heartfelt kiss.

Suniya's phone buzzed, prompting her to lift it and look at her screen.

"What is it?" Eric asked, peering over her shoulder.

"I don't know," Suniya admitted. "It looks like a message from the uni. That's weird, they normally email, not text."

She opened her phone and read the message. From her perplexed frown, Eric deduced it wasn't good news. She shook her head a few times, curling up her nose the way she does when she's perturbed.

"What did they say?" Eric inquired.

"It's about the protest today," she replied, still scowling at her phone. "I'd forgotten all about it. It's a reminder to all students that English Hearts are protesting today. 'Whilst they claim it's a peaceful protest, we are advising all students of an ethnic minority to stay indoors for their own safety.' What bullshit."

"What do you mean?"

"Well, why the hell should I have to stay indoors because a bunch of racists want to march through the town centre, chanting racist crap?"

"I'm sure it's just saying it for safety reasons," Eric assured her. "The uni just wants to make sure we're all aware."

Then Eric remembered. They had plans that evening. They were going to the pub with Beth and Max. In the centre of Hanley, near the protest.

"Maybe we should stay in?" Eric suggested, fearing any kind of conflict. "If that's what they are advising."

"No!" Suniya exclaimed, looking at Eric with horror. "Why should I? I'm not cancelling my plans. Then they've won."

"It's not about winning, Suniya, it's about being safe."

"No. I can take care of myself. Besides, we have made plans, and I am not backing out of them. These people have another thing coming if they think they are going to stop us going for our evening drinks."

Whilst Eric admired the guts his girlfriend had, he found the balance between being self-assured and putting yourself in danger precarious at best.

Still, if she really didn't think there would be a problem, why should he?

Because if someone starts on her, I'd automatically be involved.

His nerves started again. Except this time, they weren't worried nerves for meeting parents, but nerves of terror for his and Suniya's safety. What if the protest wasn't peaceful? What if something did happen? What if they were caught in the crossfire?

What if it wasn't even crossfire – what if they targeted Suniya herself?

"What's the matter?" Suniya asked, seeing the worried expression on his face.

He didn't admit what he was thinking. He knew his ridiculous cowardice irritated her. But surely, he should be honest?

"I just, I don't know. Do you really think we'll be safe?"

"Of course," she smiled lifting his arm, and leaning herself on his chest in a cosy cuddle. "After all, I've got my big, strong, strapping man with me."

It was nice of her to say.

But she was kidding herself.

Eric wasn't big and strong, and he knew it.

And as much as he admired her spirit and determination not to let these people affect her life, he couldn't help but get an awful feeling about that evening.

CHAPTER FOURTEEN

Traffic ground to a halt. Station Road filled with people pouring off the trains, prompting the police to set up cones and divert traffic elsewhere. It was chaos.

Bruno didn't care.

He was stupendously proud.

This was all because of him. The thousands of supporters flooding off the train, they were coming because he had organised them to be there.

It was a tremendous success.

And the best was still yet to come.

As Bruno made his way up Shelton Old Road toward the station, he could already hear the magnificent songs and chants of the loyal activists.

"Our England! Our England!"

"Send them home, send them home, send them home!"

"E – E – English Hearts! E – E – English Hearts!"

It reminded Bruno of a football chant, except with more diversity. This wasn't just a chorus of blokes. A mixture of voices, young and old, male and female, chimed together to make a glorious sound of unity.

This was a group of people who would make their voices heard.

As he finally reached the station, dead on time, he feasted his eyes upon the effort protestors had gone to. There were families there, parents with children cloaked in fitting outfits, such as kings and Winston Churchill. Supporters were adorned in union jack flags, draped over their shoulders, wrapped around their waist, some held around couples.

"*English Hearts, let me hear you!*" roared Bruno.

Fists raised into the air and cheers filled the street. It was victoriously deafening. Bruno's eardrums pounded with the ferocity of the volume, prompting a surge of manic glee to spread throughout his body.

Supporter after supporter greeted him, patting his back, shaking his hand, waving a joyous fist in the air in elation.

"English, English, English Hearts!" he began chanting.

And on the second time he spoke this chant, the whole street had joined in.

"English, English, English Hearts! English, English, English Hearts!"

He turned the corner and led the march down Leek Road, the incredible strength in numbers causing the traffic to have to part. Bruno felt like Moses, leading his followers through the Red Sea.

No one in the deadened traffic gave any kind of retaliation. They either stared the other way or looked to Bruno with eyes of fear.

To his right were the university halls of residence.

One of the most multicultural universities in the United Kingdom.

The reason he had chosen this place.

The reason he had hand-selected his target.

As he glared at the university, he spotted a couple crossing the car park that filled his belly with churning sickness of anger.

Hand in hand they walked, the man desperately keeping his eyes forward, and the woman turning over her shoulder to glare at the protest.

The man was white. A young, scrawny mess with glasses perched upon his face.

The woman was brown. With a headscarf wrapped around her hair, as if that meant something. Her eyes narrowed, her head slowly shaking, a venomous stare at the protest against her and her kind.

She was attractive, mind. She was slim, with a cute, rounded face, and Bruno had no doubt she had luxurious locks of hair beneath that thing she wore on her head.

But it still made him gag.

Not only was this Muslim woman plaguing his community with her presence, this white man had lowered himself to the level of dating her. He was holding her hand, his white against her brown, like snow against shit.

The woman caught his eye. Her glare lingered for a moment.

Bruno grinned. He lifted his hand to his mouth and blew her a patronising kiss.

As her head shook in disgust, he grabbed his crotch and gyrated it toward her.

She recoiled, immediately flinching away, rushing around the corner with her pathetic boyfriend.

Bruno smugly cackled.

I'll be seeing you, he thought to himself, a sinister smile spreading across his face.

I'll be seeing all of you.

He took the radio from his belt and lifted it to his mouth.

"This is Bruno Tug, come in, over," he requested.

After a few moments, the static turned to a reply.

"Hearing you, Bruno, over."

"Is everything in place? Over."

"Everything is in place, ready to go on your say so. Over."

Bruno's grin spread even wider over his face.

"ETA twenty minutes, be ready. Over and out."

"Confirmed. Over and out."

Perfect.

It was going to be a lovely day.

Consumed with happiness, he turned his focus ahead and continued leading the English Hearts, joining in with a few chants.

"We have had enough of that! We want our fucking country back! We have had enough of that! We want our fucking country back!"

CHAPTER FIFTEEN

"Are you really sure this is a good idea?" Eric insisted as he fastened the top button of his shirt.

Suniya finished buttoning her blouse and looked through her wardrobe for the perfect skirt.

Eric's jaw dropped and, for a moment, he forgot what they were talking about. Just watching her sift through her wardrobe with her silky, red underwear, sat like a crown on top of her two perfect legs, made him more than a little excitable.

He counted his lucky stars once more that this woman had devoted her time to him. She was truly beautiful. A slim body curved in all the right places, a smile that would send your heart into overdrive, and long, flowing hair that would spring over her shoulders when she let it down after a long day.

Why on earth a woman like this had ever looked his way, he didn't know. Not only was she stunning, she was a perfect mixture of confident and playful. She could make him laugh so easily, could make him feel great about himself with just a few words, and always had the courage to stand up for what she believed in.

Staring at her in that moment, he decided he never wanted

anything to change. If only he could take a picture of her and encapsulate her this way forever. That way he knew he would never lose her.

"What's not a good idea?" she prompted, putting on a long, grey, fitted skirt.

"What?" Eric's thoughts suddenly ceased as he was brought back down to earth.

"What is it about tonight that's not a good idea?"

"The protest."

Suniya rolled her eyes and turned away from him.

"Look," Eric offered, jumping to his feet and placing his arms lovingly around her. "I know you're a strong woman and all, not going to be put off by a bunch of racists – I just have a really bad feeling. Like, it's not going to be safe in town tonight."

"Eric, listen to me," she instructed, putting her arms around his neck, looking sternly and sincerely into his eyes. "I have suffered this kind of abuse since I was old enough to understand what it meant. They are a bunch of pricks, the lot of them, but they aren't going to do anything if I just ignore them. Honestly, Eric, you worry too much."

Those last few words spun around in Eric's mind.

"You worry too much."

My life in a nutshell.

So, against his better judgement, Eric held Suniya's jacket out as she placed her arms in.

And they left.

The march had already passed by the halls of residence, but its remains were left strewn across the road. Cans of lager, dropped union jack flags, even one destroyed flag of India, were left in the protest's wake.

He took her hand and clutched it tightly. Not entirely sure whether he was doing this to keep her safe, or to reassure himself, he just focussed his stare dead ahead.

They'd made it halfway down the street when they came across a group of lads sitting on a bench. They looked like teenagers. Hair greased to their foreheads, Burberry caps, and tracksuit bottoms tucked into socks. They all grinned and leered as Suniya strode past, standing up and watching her go by.

"All right love," one of them cackled.

Eric focussed dead ahead.

As did Suniya.

"Just ignore them, Eric," she whispered.

"She's lovely, can I have a go?" one of them shouted from behind them.

Don't turn around. Don't react. Just keep walking.

"Fuckin' Muslim scum! Why you wasting your time mate?" they heard another shout.

Eric wasn't sure if Suniya had heard the heckle, but hoped she hadn't.

"She's fit though, mate!"

"Can I have a go?"

"Dirty fuckin' immigrant."

Finally, they turned the corner and were out of earshot. Eric let out a big breath, glad that they were finally far enough away that he knew they wouldn't be physically attacked.

It was going to be a long night.

After fifteen minutes of walking and managing to avoid anyone else making any further derogatory remarks, they reached the pub.

Eric realised they had remained in tense silence the whole time.

"You okay?" he asked.

"I'm fine," Suniya assured him, and they entered the pub.

To say that everyone fell silent would be a tad farfetched, but that's how it felt.

Many conversations promptly ceased, and heads turned to

stare at Suniya in the doorway. A sea of white faces with their eyes fixed upon her and Eric, hand in hand, a mixed-race couple.

Not every stare was a glare. In fact, some were in shock, likely at the prospect that a Muslim woman had dared leave her house on this dreadful day.

Spotting Max and Beth in the corner, Suniya waved and, ignoring the eyes that remained on her for an uncomfortable period of time, led Eric over to them.

"How are you doing?" Beth asked, a concerned look on her face.

"Fine," Suniya replied. Eric knew her well enough to detect a slight tone of frustration at the constant requests as to her welfare, but she took it in good spirit nonetheless.

After a few minutes, eyes generally left her and people refocussed on their drinks. That was, apart from two young blokes Eric could see in the reflection of the mirror behind the bar.

Two blokes with vicious sneers pasted on their face. Pints of Stella in their hands, hoods over their heads. They did not take their eyes off Eric and Suniya the entire time they were there.

CHAPTER SIXTEEN

Jack couldn't keep his eyes off Bruno Tug.

For the entire march, the man just seemed to celebrate hate. Any racist remark, glare at a passing person who was not white-British, any new chant someone would make up that insulted numerous races, he would celebrate by kicking his head back and guffawing into the air. The rolls of fat on the back of his neck, beneath his closely shaven skinhead would jiggle as his whole body convulsed with his laughter. He stood in a constantly rigid posture, as though his oversized muscles were constricting his movement.

An oaf of a man, full of nothing but racist, violent thoughts.

He was exactly the kind of man Jack loathed.

It astounded Jack that, in this day and age, there was still a protest group that was allowed to travel to various towns and spread racist views. Not only that, but that this group had managed to attract such a substantial number of followers.

Jack looked ahead to the front of the crowd, at the long line of police officers walking in front of Bruno, leading them on their designated route. On the left and right of the buoyant, singing group, officers were spread out evenly in a line, keeping the English Hearts contained in their box.

But there still weren't enough officers. If this group decided to become violent, with the numbers they had, there was nothing Jack or any of his colleagues could do about it. Not until the riot police arrived.

Such was the precarious balance in the state of policing nowadays.

Jack was to the right of the group, toward the front, so he could maintain his surveillance on the group leader. All the work his team had put in culminated in their ability to catch this guy, and he was not about to let him out of his sight.

He knew the demonstrators were laughing at him. A black police officer at a racist protest; they probably couldn't believe their eyes.

But he didn't care.

He was glad to be stationed on this protest. It showed the English Hearts that he would not be intimidated by their presence.

He would walk alongside these racist thugs, standing proud of who he was.

A man with few teeth, a lazy eye, and a bony body, carrying a union jack flag with the person next to him, did not take his eyes off Jack.

Jack was aware of it but endeavoured to ignore it. If he rose to the glares, he would end up engaging in a confrontation, with which he would rather keep his distance.

A few years ago, he would have quite easily turned around and asked the guy, "What the hell you think you're looking at?"

But he was not there to lower himself to their level. He was there to show that he would not be deterred.

Thoughts of Tallah danced around his mind. His beautiful daughter. Something in his life worth staying safe for. Worth avoiding a risky fight for.

And Vanessa. A wonderful wife who had stuck with him through all the grief and aggravation he'd had in his job.

It wasn't worth it.

But this man's glare... It relentlessly pierced his skin. It wasn't just a lingered glance, it was an uncomfortable, menacing fixation, one that the ugly, scrawny, foul-faced man would not remove himself from.

Jack couldn't help it. Feeling the awkwardness of the situation, he turned and looked at the man, deciding that maybe an acknowledgement of this man's obsession would remove it.

The man did not look away. He just shook his head, pursing his lips, focussing his foul glare on Jack.

"You fucking darky," the man mouthed. No sound came out of his mouth, but Jack could tell well enough what the guy had said.

Jack took a big, deep breath inward, held it, then let it go.

He would not rise to it. These people were sick, horrid scumbags. Lowlifes. They weren't worth it.

"Nigger!" shouted someone from behind Jack. "Go back to Africa!"

Although he wasn't aware of who had shouted it, he was definitely aware of the laughs and cheers that followed.

Fuck them.

He turned his focus on Bruno Tug, using his hatred toward the man to distract his wary mind. As he did, he noticed something in Bruno's hand.

It was a radio.

Bruno was speaking something into the radio, then listening to the response.

Who could he be talking to?

Jack scanned the crowd, looking for someone else with a radio. The crowd went back too far for him to see everyone, but he could not see any person holding a radio in his peripheral vision.

"What you looking for, blacky?" came a voice from the crowd.

Jack ignored it and turned his focus back to Bruno.

Bruno was speaking very intently into his radio. It was more than just a "how's it going?" conversation, Jack was sure of it.

In a sudden movement, Bruno dropped the radio to his side, nodded at a man next to him, and slipped away down a side street.

Now's the time.

Jack made his way through the crowd and down the side street Bruno had slipped down, glancing one final time at his team surrounding the protest.

Little did Jack know, that final glance over his shoulder at his fellow police officers would be the last time he ever saw them.

CHAPTER SEVENTEEN

Beth and Max proved to be very good company.

The whole way through their meal and drinks, Eric was warily conscious of the looks that were being aimed in their direction. The stares were never clear or obvious but were subtle, unapparent glances. Nothing anyone could single out and, if you were to try, they could quite easily just say, "I was just looking in your direction, wasn't staring."

But he could see it.

The two lads. Sitting there. Seething at them.

One of them wore a Burberry cap, the other had his hair slathered to his forehead with an unsustainable amount of gel. They both wore tracksuits, spoke loudly, and downed Stella after Stella in the time it took Eric to finish half of his pint.

"What's the matter?" Suniya enquired, noticing Eric's attention wavering into the distance.

"Nothing, it's just," he began, then thought better of it. "Don't worry."

"Is it those guys, staring?"

"Yeah. Have you noticed?"

Suniya raised her eyebrows.

"Of course I have noticed, I'm not an idiot."

"I didn't say you were, Suniya –"

"But if I'm not bothered by them, so neither should you be. After all, it's me they are staring at, not you."

Eric went to reply but thought better of it.

She was right. They weren't staring at him. They were staring at Suniya. Eric feeling intimidated by them was ridiculous, he wasn't the Indian woman being singled out by members of a large, racist organisation whose protest gives them validation.

Then why is it I feel so worried?

Their conversation continued, engaging in rants about workload and disappointing lectures. Eventually, Eric realised he was growing a pressing need to go to the toilet.

But the toilet was across the pub.

He would have to go through the two lads to get to the men's.

He had been holding it in for a while, hoping that these two men would leave. But no, they had been drinking pint after pint and, despite not seeming to be left at all inebriated by their constant consumption of alcohol, they were still there, banging them back like they were glasses of water.

"What's the matter now?" Suniya turned to him, noticing his glances over his shoulder.

"I need the toilet," Eric weakly replied.

"Then go."

"But they are in the way."

"Oh, for goodness sake, Eric, if you need to go to the toilet, go to the toilet. They are just two men."

Red rushed to his cheeks. His embarrassed blush prompted his friends, Beth and Max, to snigger at his expense. Feeling his masculinity being questioned, he willed himself to just get up and go.

His bladder willed him.

His leg was shaking, such was his need to go to the toilet.

"Fine," he grunted, and got out of his seat.

Giving a wary glance at the two men, who weren't paying him the slightest bit of attention, he focussed his eyes dead ahead and made a beeline for the toilets.

As he pushed open the toilet door, he glanced behind himself, to see that these two men were still not paying him any attention.

I'm such a wuss.

He entered the toilet, bypassing the urinals and heading straight for a cubicle. Finding that the first cubicle had a dysfunctional lock, he made his way to the adjacent cubicle and found a sufficient bolt. Shifting it across, he turned and undid his flies.

Public toilets were a problem he'd always had, and it made him feel pathetic. He'd tried it a few times, standing at a urinal. He'd even managed to start peeing once – but then a man came and stood next to him, and he'd completely stopped midstream.

It was a ridiculous anxiety, and not one he'd be particularly willing to admit to Suniya.

But, as he had found that a cubicle allowed him to lock himself in, and encouraged by the lack of noise outside the cubicle door, he finished peeing and pulled his zip up.

That's when he heard them.

The toilet room door swinging open and needlessly thrashing against the wall beside it. Two heavy footsteps marching in, accompanied by the voices he had only heard from afar, gloating and cocky.

"Ah, mate, ah need a fuckin' slash."

"Ah've been savin' this piss up for fuckin' ages."

Shit.

What was he going to do?

What do I mean, what am I going to do? For Christ's sake Eric, you are a grown man. You are going to leave the cubicle, wash your hands, and go back to your drinks.

Willing himself to just leave the cubicle, urging his body forward, his hand failed him. It shook as he gripped the lock, making the door shake with it.

Now he had shaken the door, they would know he was there.

He had no choice. He would have to leave now.

Taking a huge, inward breath, he departed the cubicle and took four precise, definite steps to the sink.

At the same time, almost as if fate was colluding against him, the two blokes finished their business and joined the sinks either side of him.

His arms shook. His heart raced. He was in the middle of them, aware of the glances they were throwing his way.

Then one of them spoke.

His breath caught in his throat.

"Eh, y'all right mate?" the first bloke asked.

Eric forced an introverted smile and took his focus back to his hands.

"You're the geezer in the corner, ain't yuh? Havin' a drink with those other three?" the man persisted.

"Yep," Eric forced out, though he wasn't sure whether he'd spoken loud enough for them to hear.

"Ah, ma god, yes, mate," interjected the second bloke. "Ah was watchin' you."

"You're with that paki bird, ain't you?" the first bloke eagerly enquired.

Eric flinched at the word 'Paki,' but forced his face not to show it. The word filled him with dread, a pain for what Suniya went through he could never put into words.

But he didn't want to cause trouble.

So he said nothing.

He let them say it. Let them call her by the word that completely degrades and offends her entire culture.

Because he wasn't man enough to stand up to it.

"Mate, what's the deal with that?" the second bloke leant against the sink, intently leaning forward with eager eyes.

"Yeah, what, you fuckin' her?" the first asked.

Eric stifled a faint nod, not wanting to respond, fearing what they might do if he said yes.

"What's the matter, can't talk? She your bird or what?"

"Yes," Eric softly forced out. "She is."

"Whoa!" the bloke screeched with his cackle. "How the fuck did that happen? What, you lose a bet?"

Eric paused, feeling their stares, and forced a headshake.

"Then why you datin' a paki bird?"

Eric shrugged his shoulders.

The blokes' teasing demeanour dropped, and their eyes went intently serious. Their playful toying with him faded to sinister glares.

"Answer the fuckin' question, mate, why you datin' a paki bird?"

Eric closed his eyes. Willed himself to think of something to say. Something that would satisfy them, but still let him keep an ounce of integrity.

"Excuse me," he coughed, and rushed out of the room, heading to the door in such a sudden motion they wouldn't be able to do anything to stop him.

As he sat down at the table, feeling the glares on the back of his head, he did not turn his head once to look at them.

He did not dare.

CHAPTER EIGHTEEN

KARL SAT AT HIS COMPUTER, unnoticed and unneeded, just like every other day of his life.

People strode and dashed past his cubicle, but never so much as looked at him. They went to visit their friend's cubicles, and Karl would watch as they laughed and joked and made merry idle conversation.

Karl did none of this.

He had no friends on Facebook, no emails from colleagues, and no invitations to any social events.

Except for one set of friends.

The set of friends he was waiting avidly for a text message from.

As he did, his head slumped on his hand, his eyes glazing over the dismal setting of his nine-to-five job. Grey walls and faded cream ceilings, with stained brown blinds blocking out the blinding sun in the beautiful sky. The carpet was engrained with crumbs and fluff, to the point that the wheels of his chair struggled to move.

It was a miserable place. And he hated it.

The work ended. And he had to go home.

Back to the only cheap bedsit he could afford, cold pizza in the fridge, and a television that still had the big back.

Then his phone buzzed.

And his hand elatedly grabbed it, turning the screen toward him.

He had a message. Who was it from?

Bruno Tug.

"Yes!" He pumped his fist into the air in celebration. Then, realising he may have just shown too much excitement, he looked around himself to see if anyone had seen.

Of course, they hadn't.

He opened the text message.

"Deploy ShutDown8."

Perfect.

He finally got to do it.

He had been working on ShutDown8 for almost a year, waiting in heated anticipation for when he could finally use it. Now was the time. It was like the Christmas Eve wait was over; it was Christmas Day, and he could finally open his presents.

No.

This was better.

He opened the browser and copied and pasted the address for the government office's internal directory, entering the passwords he had previously prepared. To be able to implement a task with such ease had taken a year's worth of hacking, as well as creating and developing individual, distinct programs; so he was delighted to see that it had all paid off.

Not that he had ever doubted it would.

These programs could have earned thousands on the black web, paying off his debts in a heartbeat.

But he had chosen to use them for something greater, and now it was time for the real test of their aptitude.

Entering safe browser mode, he tinkered with the proxy server and accessed a screenshot of an individual computer, using his amended version of a software program called Impero. It had taken him weeks to tweak the coding and turn this apt piece of software into a unique hacking program.

I should be getting paid far more than this dickish company is paying me.

It was true.

But he couldn't get a better job. Otherwise, they would know what he could do.

And they would find him before he could complete his mission.

After waiting for the computer he was monitoring to become stationary, he hit the *control* button.

His next actions had to be quick. The computer's operator may only be on a coffee or bathroom break, and he didn't have long.

He opened a program entitled Electronic Magnetic Global Positioning Tracking. Pressing the right buttons, he led himself to a screen flow that would allow him to grab every phone number currently switched on in the city of Stoke-on-Trent.

Within half a minute, he had exported this as a spreadsheet to his own computer and relinquished control of the government desktop, no one the wiser.

Opening his own email, he imported the list of phone numbers into the TO section of a draft message.

Then he attached it. The ShutDown8 file.

He wrote *Hello old friend!* in the body of the message.

It was ready.

The virus was there. Every phone number in the target location was there.

Now all he had to do was click send.

With a knowing look, he scanned the room.

All these ungrateful sycophants who ignored him every day. All these spongers who never gave a shit about anyone but themselves.

They were about to find out just what he could do.

"Fuck you," he quietly declared, and clicked send.

CHAPTER NINETEEN

JACK KNEW he was being followed.

The man had been incredibly unsubtle.

For the whole walk in the path of Bruno Tug, the same messy footsteps had echoed quietly in the distance behind him. The same reflection of an upturned collar and a cap pulled down appeared in every shop window.

It didn't scare him.

He had his hand on his asp, ready.

Whatever racist prick had followed him back from the march would get what was coming to them. He wasn't about to take any more grief.

Feeling a vibration against his hip, he withdrew his phone. It wasn't an opportune moment, but it could be Tallah.

But it wasn't.

It was a text message. From an unrecognised email address. Someone had sent him a text from their computer.

How odd.

The subject line read *Hello old friend!*

It could be anyone. Or, it could be important.

Glancing up to ensure he still had sights on Bruno Tug, he opened the text message to see what it was about.

It was blank.

But within an instant of the text being opened, his phone screen turned into a chaotic scramble. Messy waving lines and random colours wiped up and down the screen.

Then they stopped and settled on one final image.

The English Hearts logo.

Why has someone sent me this?

He hit the home button, trying to leave this screen. It did nothing. He tried to power off, but it still did nothing.

He bashed every button, held down every escape shortcut he knew, and knocked the phone against his leg.

It did nothing.

The screen was stuck, in an everlasting, frozen image of their target.

The phone was completely unusable.

Was someone trying to taunt them?

Then it came. Lingering from nearby. Warm burning, choking him, spreading through his nostrils, filling him with alarm.

He lifted his head.

That was when he saw it.

His heart punched and punched his ribs, his lungs taking in air quicker and quicker.

Smoke.

Rising into the air, creating a cloudy mixture of grey and black. Consuming the air with a potent smell of flames he couldn't ignore.

Coming from the direction he was walking.

The direction of the police station.

Without hesitation, he broke into a run. The footsteps behind him grew faster too, but he didn't care. He sprinted as quickly as he could.

As the flickering of the flames came slowly into view, he tripped over and went flying onto his front. As he turned to see what had tripped him, his stomach churned out a mouthful of sick.

A young police officer.

A trainee.

Gormless eyes stared vacantly up at Jack with an overwhelming absence of life.

Jack's head pounded against his skull, his forehead throbbing, alarm furiously beating his mind.

He sprinted forward.

It was too late.

The police station was a crumbling mess of a building, consumed by flames that lashed out so furiously, ash landed at his feet. The heat reached out for him and grabbed his throat, choking him on its dirty smoke.

A few yards away, a group of men with scarves tied around their heads and collars lifted over cheap tracksuits held firebombs in their hands.

Laughing together, they lifted bottles with lit tissues sticking out of the end and threw them at the station with all the strength they had.

The bottles only added to the flames, causing another thrash into the air.

"*Stop!*" screamed Jack, not even aware he had opened his mouth. Before he knew it, he was charging at these hooligans, his face wrapped up in a venomous snarl, seeing nothing but red.

He didn't reach them.

He fell to the ground in a mighty clatter, smacking his nose into the concrete.

Lifting himself up, groggily croaking as he tasted blood, he realised the back of his head was in an immense amount of pain.

I've been hit. Something has hit me.

THWACK!

Once again, something solid and firm lunged itself into the lower back of his skull. Wooden splinters pricked out of his head, forcing Jack to endure a prolonged wave of pain.

Jack dizzily slumped back onto his front.

He knew he needed to keep conscious.

He had no idea what was happening. Didn't understand who was doing what. But it didn't matter.

Need to keep my eyes open.

Someone's cackling faded into a high-pitch ring. The floor before him was vague chaos, blurred into various colours, with a hazy orange blur flickering in the near distance.

Jack felt a subdued high come over him. A chaotic clarity, an unclear awareness.

He rolled over and slumped onto his back, breaking into a coughing fit. The taste of blood consumed his mouth, forcing him to dribble thick, red gunk down his cheek.

"What..." he forced, finding it hard to speak. "Who..."

A hand reached into his mouth, cupping the top of his jaw. A frantic moan of agony fell from his lips as he felt himself dragged across the ground.

Instinctively, Jack shut his teeth together, biting into the fingers with all his might.

A scream of pain echoed and took Jack a few moments to realise it wasn't him.

THUMP!

Jack was on his side in an instant.

Pressing his eyes together in a flinch of pain, he realised a boot had been planted into the side of his head, retaliation to him clamping his teeth together.

A few more strikes landed on the side of his head, and all Jack could do was scrunch up his face and take it.

He tried to lift his arms, but his muscles failed him.

He tried to speak, but his voice turned into a vacant whimper.

He tried to look at the man who was attacking him, but his vision was too unfocused.

He could feel himself slipping away.

His mind rested on the image of Vanessa's face. That beautiful face, still as beautiful as the day he first saw her. The feeling of placing his arms around her waist, of feeling her soft lips pressed gently against his, her smooth skin caressing his body.

Tallah.

His daughter. Two years old. A gift.

No, he would not give in. He would not let his failing muscles stay rooted to the floor. He would not let his whimpering voice remain void of screaming. He would not let his vision remain unfocused.

As he reached up, his teeth gritted into an aggressive snarl, going for the man who had attacked him, something harshly planted itself into the back of his head.

Then it all went blank.

CHAPTER TWENTY

THE SOFT TOUCH of Suniya's hand felt nice. Such things still made Eric immensely happy. The simple act of a gentle hand in his made his anxieties seem distant.

Except, in that moment, her hand was no longer gentle.

It gripped him so tightly he could feel her fingers digging into his bones. But he didn't care, as he was doing the same. He clutched onto her for dear life, wanting to make sure she was still close, ensuring she was safe.

A blinding white light filled the pub first, consuming the air with a rising grey smoke. Rumbles of an explosion followed, prompting a mass panic. Every single person was out of their seats, frantically searching for cover. Some grabbed hold of their loved ones, some clung onto each other, and some just ran aimlessly with nowhere to go.

Everyone, that was, apart from the two men who had taunted Eric in the toilet. They stayed still, sipping on the last of their beers, grinning knowingly.

Eric's mind was a disordered mess. Both he and Suniya looked around the room, trying to think of what they should do.

Looking at Suniya, Eric felt a sudden sting of love, a need to protect her, an abrupt longing to keep her safe, whatever it took.

Now's no time to be your cowardly self, Eric. Man up. Keep her safe.

Before he could make sense of his thoughts and rationalise a coherent plan, multiple windows were smashed and various parts of the pub were launched into flames.

A table in the far corner turned to rapid fire. The spilt alcohol along the bar engulfed it into a monstrous blaze.

"Come on!" Eric shouted to Suniya. Grabbing hold of her hand as tightly as he could, he took her to the pub door and peered out the window.

The pub was surrounded.

Multiple hooligans clad in balaclavas and scarves that concealed their repulsive identities stood with bottles alight with fire. A man stepped forward, a megaphone attached to his mouth.

"This is your warning!" he shouted. "Give us any Muslims, and we will leave your pub alone! I repeat, give up any Muslims, and all white people will go free!"

Eric's wide, terrified eyes turned to the rest of the pub.

Everyone was pressed up against the walls of the pub, the only salvation from the flames licking at their heels. They stared dead-eyed toward Suniya.

Suniya, the only Muslim in the pub.

Caucasian eyes wickedly glaring back at her.

Eric clutched onto her hand, making his way in front of her, acting as a barrier between him and them.

His arms shook, his legs practically seized, but instinct took over. As horrified as he was, it would only take one or two of them to give her up.

"I think you need to step outside," came the low, croaky voice of the barman, an elderly Scottish man peering down his nose at Suniya.

Another firebomb crashed through a far window and an innocent woman's leg set alight. This woman's partner instantly took a glass of water and hurled it over her, dabbing on the flickering flames.

This man turned over his shoulder at Suniya and Eric.

"Get the fuck out of the pub," he demanded.

"We aren't going anywhere," Eric grunted into Suniya's ear, looking around for an escape.

Suniya's wide, mortified eyes gazed back at him, filling with tears. No longer concealing her crushingly terrified eyes.

"Come on," Eric demanded.

Taking her hand, he dragged her across the pub, away from the volatile hoard who'd been edging closer to them. Dodging the flames, Eric barged open the back door of the pub and fell through it, taking Suniya with him.

As he looked over his shoulder, he scowled at the crowd of angry people who had been innocently enjoying their drinks a moment ago.

Eric took a plank of discarded wood fallen from a crate of beer and slipped it through the door handles, halting the barges of the angry mob that pursued them.

Eric turned to the backroom, considering their options, aware of the repeated banging against the door behind him.

"What do we do?" Suniya wept.

Eric looked around. This was a cooled room, with boxes of beer, and a narrow passage between the stored bottles.

"We keep going," he reassured her. "This way."

He dragged her further forward, ignoring her tears, willing her to be the strong woman she was. They made their way around the corner of the room, found a fire exit, and barged through.

They stumbled through the door and landed on the floor of a wet, harsh alleyway, the crumbles of the pavement cutting their knees.

The alarm of the fire exit instantly belted out, and Eric knew they couldn't stay in this alleyway for long.

But the only other way out of the alleyway was back the way they came, so he allowed the door to slam shut behind him.

He could see the hooligans who had bombarded the pub turning their attention toward the sound of the alarm. Eric and Suniya were concealed in shadow for the moment, but soon the attackers would come down the alleyway and they would have nowhere to go.

Eric suddenly realised how much he was shaking. His knees were bashing against each other. Any unexpected surge of valiant thinking he had felt moments ago was gone.

He was terrified.

The adrenaline coursing through his body did nothing to halt his fear.

It was fight or flight.

And he was pretty good at flight.

I am pretty good at running away. And right now, we need to run away.

"Eric?" Suniya whimpered beside him. "We're trapped."

He wrapped his arms around her and held her close, peering into the distance, watching the figures move closer, the angry glow of orange fire illuminating them.

They were making their way toward the alleyway.

Behind Eric and Suniya was a dead end.

They were coming toward them.

Eric looked around himself, desperately searching for something.

The only thing they could do was hide.

A group of dumpsters were propped up against the end of the alleyway. Grabbing Suniya's hand, he dragged her further into the alley and manoeuvred them both into a position behind the dumpsters.

Eric propped himself into the small space, squashed

between the dumpster and the wall, pressed against the foul stench of stale alcohol and manky cheese and onion crisps.

In front of him, Suniya was equally squashed. As they pressed against each other to ensure they would not be seen, Eric put his arms around her, covering her mouth with one of his hands.

Heavy footsteps splashed through the puddles that lay at the entrance to the alleyway.

Eric only just realised it was raining.

"Swore I fuckin' saw 'em, mate," Eric heard a voice snarl.

A mumbled voice replied, stifled by the concealment of their face disguise.

A few more heavy footsteps announced themselves in the alleyway.

Eric tried to count how many there were, but he couldn't be sure. But, from the sight of the muddy shoes visible beneath the dumpster, there were at least five.

Five arsonists hunting the woman held closely in his arms.

He withdrew his phone. Maybe he could text someone to help, let someone know. Anything.

But the moment he looked at his phone screen, he knew it would be no good.

The screen was stuck on a frozen image of the English Hearts logo. He did everything he could to get rid of it – bashed the phone against his legs, hit every button. It was no good.

Reaching into Suniya's pocket, he grabbed her phone.

It was exactly the same.

It was this discovery that caused Eric to speculate as to just how widely the attack had gone, and just how helpless they were.

They were on their own.

"All right boys," came a cocky voice, entering the alleyway.

From the small crack beneath the dumpster, Eric peered

out, watching as fragments of the scene loosely revealed themselves. The face of an Indian man appeared, falling heavily into a mixture of hard cement and muddy puddles. A hefty, black boot pressed down on the man's head.

"What we gonna do with 'im, Bruno?" came another voice, with a tone of overwhelmed respect.

"Mate," replied the man referred to as Bruno. "I am gonna string him up by his bollocks and leave him to burn."

CHAPTER TWENTY-ONE

Karl kept glancing at the door and back to his email. At the door and back to his email.

He knew it wouldn't be long until he was discovered.

They could easily track who hacked into the government computer. They could easily figure out where it came from, and which computer did it. His hacking software was impressive, but it wasn't impenetrable; a life as a hacker will teach you that nothing is.

So he just had to sit and wait.

Sit and hope that Bruno's subsequent text would arrive first.

As he waited, he set two pairs of scissors on the desk beneath him, perfectly and precisely.

All around him, he watched as people took out their phones and cursed. Around the office people continuously pressed buttons, tried turning their phone off, hit them against the table. Every cubicle, the same frustration.

It made Karl laugh to know that he did this and they were all clueless.

Fucking idiots.

He even laughed out loud at a woman furiously trying to

switch her phone off, knowing that no one would pay him the slightest bit of attention. It was a bloody good virus he'd made – she would not be doing anything with that phone again.

Then the email came through.

A blank email simply reading *deploy* in the subject line.

"Right you are, Bruno," Karl gleefully confirmed, knowing that no one would notice or care.

This part was a bit trickier, but he loved a challenge.

There was nothing he couldn't hack.

He selected the Trojan an acquaintance had deployed on his behalf, and within seconds had put it into his self-made program and opened a folder entitled Public Utilities that displayed the IP addresses he had gathered in the past few weeks. He probed the connections, searching for access until he finally found the login dialog for Western Power Distribution. Using the system ports information he had bought from a disgruntled employee, he clicked a few buttons, and he was in.

He dragged the icon for his virus across the screen and dropped it into the program. Within seconds, every IP address he had for Western Power Distribution's computers and servers were irreparably changed.

It took a matter of minutes until he had done this for every company serving Stoke-on-Trent. Npower, British Gas, EDF, First Utility, Scottish Power, Extra Energy, OVC Energy – all of them. Even the small businesses serving the area were hit.

Once he had control of each server, he dragged the malware and placed it on their systems. He had designed it perfectly – so it would hit their control centre, their substations, and their communications infrastructure all at the exact same time.

A year he had waited to use this piece of malware, constantly updating it to make sure it would work, and now here it was. Working perfectly.

He sat back in his chair, lifted his hands as if preparing for rapturous applause, and then...

Everything went dark. The lights, the computers, the monitors. The whole office was plunged into black.

Honks from cars at the base of the office building screamed as failing traffic lights caused multiple collisions.

He had done it.

And, as two uniformed policemen appeared at the far entrance, he knew it was just in time.

He stood, grinning at them.

"Are you here for me?" Karl enquired.

"Are you Karl Jenkins?" one of them prompted as they approached his desk.

Without hesitating, Karl grabbed the two pairs of scissors he had readied and plunged them into the throats of the two officers before him.

Screams rang out, shrieks and wails of shock and horror as these two officers fell to their knees, clutching their neck as blood seeped through their fingers.

Karl chuckled as he even heard one person shout, "Phone an ambulance!"

Fat chance of that happening.

But there was one final thing.

If he was caught, they could make him return everything he'd done. They could torture him until he did it.

So he ran toward the open window at the end of the row of cubicles. Leaping onto the table first, he dove through the narrow crack and flew to the ground beneath him, plummeting thankfully to his death.

CHAPTER TWENTY-TWO

SCREAMS ECHOED in Jack's mind. He knew he'd been knocked unconscious somehow. But he was too groggy and too dizzily unaware to fully understand the situation he was in.

As he tried to move his hands he found them restrained behind his back. Handcuffs dug harshly into his wrists, a constant discomfort he couldn't escape.

It was at this point he realised they were his own handcuffs.

Lifting his head and slowly blinking his eyes, he willed his vision to return to focus.

His head pounded. Distant explosions thumped the forefront of his mind, whilst nearby screams punched the rest.

"Don't come any fuckin' closer," came an antagonistic man's voice close to Jack's ear.

His vision came to in blurs. A grey gravel surface beneath him came into focus, as did occasional white markings.

He was on a road. He was sure of that.

Lifting his head to his side, he saw a line of people, metres away from each other. All of them were on their knees.

The crumbling stones of the ground dug into his kneecaps. He was on his knees too.

Looking down, he noticed the frayed holes of his trousers. The uniform he had spent so many years taking care of, destroyed without remorse.

That's when he realised the rest of the people on their knees were also police officers. Some he recognised. Some, he even knew.

None of them looked up.

All of them wept, the protective facade they displayed to the public dropped. No fight left in any of them. Their uniforms ripped and their dignity torn.

Some sobbed. Some spat blood. Some were too hazy to even realise where they were, their heads spinning in a drugged-up blur.

"If you do not let these people go," came a commanding voice before him. "We will be forced to open fire."

A gun clicked next to his ear.

The view before Jack became clear. Soldiers. Privates. Generals. Sergeants of all ranks, stood with their guns pointed forward. There were at least twenty of them.

A sudden sigh of relief exuded from Jack. He was saved. He was going to be okay. There was no way these people could outnumber them.

"You back off," came the voice from behind him. "Or we will start killing little piggies."

Jack forcefully blinked, starting to finally comprehend the situation. How were these people not surrendering?

A glance over his shoulder explained everything.

Hooligans after hooligans stood down the road behind him, farther than he could see, their faces concealed, adorned with guns and knives. Some officers were dead already, left strewn across the stained pavement beneath the feet of the perpetrators.

"We repeat–" began the army general.

Three gunshots echoed so loudly they deafened Jack. A

ringing echoed so loudly in his head he didn't even hear himself shouting, bellowing that resulted in the butt of a gun being smashed into his cranium.

Along the line of officers, three more dead men now lay on the floor.

"If you do not back off, we will shoot more," came a sinister, determined voice behind Jack.

The army general gave a signal to his men. They dropped their guns.

Slowly, they backed away.

What?

Jack couldn't believe it.

What are you doing? Don't go! Save us!

It was no good.

The piece of hope Jack had clung to was fading away. The army surrendered, giving these thugs control.

Jack turned his head and looked up at the man who held a gun to his head.

Upon the man's chest, over the man's heart, was a symbol, engrained into his clothes.

The symbol for English Hearts.

The protest group.

How had they done this?

How had they the resources? The weapons? The coordination? The ability? The know-how? The expertise?

This was ridiculous.

How had no intelligence been picked up? How had no one known they were planning this?

So much time monitoring our enemies abroad, a new threat had been allowed to grow at home. Men inspired by England's enemies, working in the shadows at home.

It was clever, really.

Psychotic, destructive, scary – but clever.

And here he was, a black officer, with a gun pointed to his head. Other officers already dying.

How much chance did he have?

The man behind him picked up a radio and confirmed something Jack couldn't make out.

"Get the ones we don't need, instructions are to take them to Trentham," he commanded the other perpetrators.

A man's hand clenched around Jack's arm, hoisting him up and shoving him forward.

If Jack didn't do something soon, make some kind of attempt to escape, they would kill him.

Problem is, if he attempted to escape, they would kill him.

The whole time, there were only two thoughts shooting around his head.

Vanessa.

Tallah.

CHAPTER TWENTY-THREE

Suniya did her best to ignore the constant pains in her side. She and Eric were pressed up against each other, sandwiched between the wall, the dumpster, and the floor. The wheel of the dumpster scraped her ribs, and her arms were bruised against the pressure of the bumpy surface.

But she had to endure it.

She had to.

If she made a sound, she... well, she had no idea what they would do. How far they would go.

The whole time, she stared through the gap beneath the dumpster, knowing Eric was doing the same.

There were at least eight of them now, from the sight of their feet. All of them spoke aggressively and seemed to idolise the one they kept referring to as Bruno.

And then there was the Indian man.

He lay on the floor, his tears mixing with the dirty puddles, his face a mixture of blood and mud.

A big, chubby hand with fat fingers took hold of the back of the man's hair and lifted him up until all she could see was the dangling of this man's feet.

"What's your name?" grunted the voice of Bruno.

The man wept.

"I said what's your name? I can't keep callin' you fuckin' paki boy, can I? That's rude!"

Sniggers filled the alleyway.

Suniya felt sick.

This man. This poor, poor man. Being abused and humiliated.

For being of Indian origin.

Just like Suniya.

Just like Suniya's family.

She stifled a breath, unaware she was trembling, and felt Eric's hand push against her mouth. As much as it hurt, she was grateful for it – she could not let herself make a sound.

"Ahmad," whimpered the man.

"'Course it fuckin' is! What are you, Ahmad, a fuckin' Muslim or what?"

"Yes!" cried the man. "I am! Please, I have a wife and a child."

"Yeah, I bet you do," Bruno pleasurably moaned. "Don't worry, Ahmad. We'll get to them yet."

A sudden thwack of a jaw against brick caused Suniya to flinch, watching a tooth drop against the floor with a silent echo.

"Please, let me go! I haven't done anything to hurt you!"

"Nothin' to hurt us? What about the fuckin' Twin Towers, eh? What about 7/7, and all that? What about fuckin' ISIS?"

"They have nothing to do with me!"

"Yes they do, they are fuckin' Muslim, so are you! You're all fuckin' scum, the lot of yuh."

Another slam into the wall prompted another few teeth to clatter against the ground.

More punches were heard, more swipes, more attacks, all blending into one wave of volatile noise.

A single droplet of blood glistened in the moonlight as it splashed into a puddle below.

The man's face fell against the floor. Suniya recoiled at the sight of a nose broken to the side, a cut down the face, and numerous teeth hanging off.

For a moment, Ahmad saw Suniya.

They made eye contact.

Ahmad's eyes filled with tears. Desperate, painful tears, reaching out to Suniya.

She felt his pain. She could see it in his brown eyes; all his terror, his worry.

Ahmad knew this was it, and Suniya could see that, all in one mere, fleeting glance.

A thick knee landed with a thud beside Ahmad, next to a large, intimidating boot with sinisterly clicking buckles.

The fat hand of the man Suniya presumed was Bruno slowly shifted downwards, revealing a large knife. This wasn't any average kitchen knife – this was a large, curved, sharp hunting blade one would only buy with intention to use it.

"I need to make an example out of you, Ahmad."

"No..."

"I need to show this city what we intend to do."

"Please..."

"I need to cut you up and hang your insides high so high everyone can see 'em. So everyone can see that, before this night is through, we will have rid the city of your scum."

"Don't..."

"You are not welcome in our country."

"I am British... I was born here..."

The hand clenched harder around the knife in constant fury, reacting to Ahmad's final words with severe hatred.

In a swipe so fast Suniya wasn't even sure she saw it, Bruno's knife stuck into Ahmad's throat. Bruno held the knife there,

Ahmad's vacant eyes widening then flattening, his arms weakly lifting in a plea to let him go, then sinking into a puddle.

As his breath turned to absent chokes, Bruno swiped the knife out of Ahmad's throat and took a step back.

Ahmad's head turned to the side, locking eye contact with Suniya. His arms clambered to his wound, trying to apply pressure, trying to do something about it.

But there was nothing he could do.

He struggled for breath. He clambered for oxygen that never came, clinging to his last moments of life.

Then he was still.

His arms no longer thrashed, his lungs no longer tried.

His eyes were left wide open, fixed on Suniya's. His cold, dead eyes, staring into hers, seeing what he was no longer able to see.

Eric had to hold his hand to Suniya's mouth tighter than he had done, doing all he could to stop her weeping, stop her crying out, stop her gasping.

Sick filled her mouth, and it poured out between Eric's fingers, dripping down his sleeve.

Still, Eric did not falter.

He kept his hand clenched tightly over her lips.

The men cheered.

Congratulations were eagerly bestowed upon Bruno for his courage and willingness to make the difference.

"Go. Do the same. Kill any you see."

With Bruno's words ringing in their minds, his minions fled. Eric watched as the footsteps grew distant, runs and cheers echoing into the vague cries of the night.

Nothing was left in the alley but Eric, Suniya, and Ahmad.

That's when he let his grip on her go.

She flung her arms around him, squeezing him, clutching onto him, holding him as tightly as she could.

They were alone.

And they were being hunted.

Suniya tried closing her eyes, but it was still there. The dead eyes of Ahmad left stranded in the alleyway.

STAFFORDSHIRE TIMES
WIDE-SPREAD ATTACK ACROSS MULTICULTURAL TOWN OF STOKE-ON-TRENT

The country is in meltdown this evening. Every person stands in disbelief at the events unfolding on our very doorsteps.

What began as a peaceful protest by the anti-Islamic group English Hearts turned into violence within the space of twenty minutes. Police stations have been left in flames, mosques in tatters, and dead bodies line the streets.

The army has attempted to enter the city, only to be met by representatives of English Hearts holding police officers hostage. Forced to retreat, the army took with them the English Hearts' demands.

No helicopters. No army. No entrance to the city whatsoever.

And, to show they mean business, an estimated upwards of forty officers have been executed in front of the army's very eyes, upon their initial refusal to back off.

Electricity has gone down in the area and it appears phones have been shut down by a well-crafted, but prolific, virus. There is, as it stands, no way for anyone to contact people within the city.

We can only hope that a solution is brought forward quickly. The prime minister has already returned from holiday, saying, "We will be meeting with the head of the Metropolitan police and the army, with intention of making a plan to remove these tyrants from our city streets. Make no mistake – they are not in control."

As comforting as the prime minister's words may be, they do not appear to be true. With the prime minister currently meeting the demands of Bruno Tug, the leader of the English Hearts, the government appears helpless. Fearing the loss of hostage life and victims within the city, the prime minister has also confirmed that they will not be entering Stoke-on-Trent in the coming hours.

People across the country are asking – how did we let this threat go unnoticed? These people, manipulating their way into the various sections of our society based on hate, have turned out to be a bigger threat than any terrorist ever has been.

It looks like, for now, Stoke-on-Trent is on their own.

Our prayers go with you.

CHAPTER TWENTY-FOUR

Scars are a dignified way of telling people not to fuck with you.

Pearson loved his scar. Like the way a woman might treasure a necklace given to her by a childhood lover, or a doting man might treasure his wedding ring. His scar was his piece of treasure that he kept safe.

Always proud to display it.

People would always stare. They couldn't help it, such was its prominence.

Honestly, he got a little turned on by the flinching looks of fear.

That sudden widening of someone's eyes when they saw it, then quickly averted attention so as not to offend him.

Fuck offending him.

He loved it.

And its pain as he woke up mid-afternoon only reminded him of the pain he was to inflict that day. His back was sore from the metallic bed he'd rested on. This hotel reminded him of prison. The confined walls, the discomfort of a narrow, single bed.

People are usually terrified of going to prison.

Those people are idiots.

A television, an Xbox, a kettle. All in one room. What else does anyone need?

Outside, he had to steal and deceive for his money. As enthralling as it was, prison was just easy.

And the conjugal visits with whatever whore Bruno had bought him showed loyalty. Showed there was something waiting for him on the outside. Bruno still took care of him, even when he had been sent under.

That's because Bruno was proud of him.

For what he had done. For the destruction he'd left on disgraceful bastards who don't belong in this country.

Fuck those people.

And fuck his country for thinking they could punish him for it.

Punish him?

That cell was the best holiday he'd ever had.

People inside feared him like he was a wild lion. He ruled them. He beat the shit out of them, and there was nothing anyone could do to stop him.

They kept Muslims off his cell block because he was a danger to them. It kept his cell block clean. Kept it as he liked it.

Then they tried taking his television away to punish him.

Fifty prisoners on the cell block and two prison guards thought they could get away with that.

They put up a fight.

And gave him the scar he was so proud of.

But they regretted it.

And they never fucked with him again. No matter what he did, whom he bullied, whom he decided he owned – the prison officers couldn't do shit.

Because he'd kill them.

And they knew it.

He wouldn't even have hesitated.

And now the day had come. It was the day he had been waiting for. His beloved Stoke-on-Trent would be given back to him. Back to the British. Back to the loyal locals.

Back to the people who belonged to this once-great country.

Peeling the curtains back, Pearson feasted his eyes upon the carnage below.

It had already begun.

There was justice in the air. And it felt so good.

Watching scumbags dragged out of their homes and shown where they belong. Death, blood, torture – it filled the streets like his veins filled with adrenaline.

He felt giddy.

Like a kid on Christmas morning.

It was time. It was here.

Bruno was expecting him.

And Pearson was not about to let Bruno down.

CHAPTER TWENTY-FIVE

THE NUMB EYES of Ahmad crusted with mud. The rain pulverised his body, splashing grime from the puddle against his lifeless face.

Eric watched Suniya, unable to move.

He couldn't watch the body. He had to watch Suniya.

But, if anything, watching her was harder.

She couldn't move her eyes away from Ahmad. Even as the weather attacked the body into hazy submission, her eyes still fixated on the lifeless corpse left strewn across the floor. Humiliated in death, for being the same ethnicity as her.

Eric could see what she was thinking.

Is this what will happen to her?

If she was caught, would they disgrace her? Humiliate her? Kill her?

Eric knew the answer.

He knew Suniya knew it, too.

But they had to move.

"Suniya," Eric whispered. "They are gone."

Suniya slowly rotated her head toward Eric, her bloodshot eyes torn open.

"We need to—" Suniya started, realising she didn't know the answer to that sentence. What did they need to do?

Eric looked around for some kind of salvation. Some place they could go, escape, be safe.

All he got was harsh droplets of water bombarding his face, water so cold it seared him. The frozen wall that sandwiched them against the dumpster dug into his spine. His back and his legs were drenched with muddy water, thick with the dirt of the street and the stench of the dumpsters.

He hadn't even noticed that stench. Somehow, it had mixed with the fine smell of rain.

But he noticed it now. It hit him with frenzied alarm. A frenzied alarm that told them they needed to move.

"This looks like a flat block," Suniya pointed out, looking at the building the opposite side of the alleyway to the pub. "We could hide there. Phone the police."

Eric didn't have the heart to tell her the phones weren't working.

Suniya fumbled to her feet, pressing her bruised palms against the wall, pushing herself up. Her hands rested against the dumpster as she attempted to keep her balance.

Eric also dragged himself up, holding onto the dumpster. He didn't realise his legs had gone numb from holding Suniya so tightly until he tried to use them. Almost instantly they gave way, and Suniya put a hand out to try and steady him.

After a struggle, they both rested against the back of the dumpster, peering through the alleyway.

The thick cloak of the night had descended, and the only illumination came from moonlight and the amber glow of nearby fires. They expected to see street-lamps showing them the end of the alleyway, but there was no such guidance. No respite from the darkness, no route for them to take.

"How do we know no one's there?" Eric whispered.

"We don't," Suniya acknowledged. "But we can't stay here. They'll find us."

"They will find us in the building—"

Suniya shot her head around to Eric and whispered with aggressive venom in her voice, "I am not sitting here, staring at the dead face of a man they killed because of his heritage. I am not having it. They will come back to this alleyway, and they will find us. We need somewhere better to hide."

Eric stared at her, motionless, at a loss of what to say. His head spun with undesirable fates.

What if they are waiting at the end of the alleyway?

What if there are loads of them there?

"I—" Eric stuttered.

"No, Eric," Suniya continued. "I'm not going to sit around and wait for them to kill me. We are creeping around the front and going into that building. Okay?"

Eric's eyes lingered over Suniya for a solemn moment. Her hijab, so brightly coloured, faded to a brown, wet mess. Tears escaping her eyes got lost in the rain, mixing with the abyss of absence.

He needed to understand how she felt.

It wasn't him they were after.

It was her.

Because of who she was. Because of her skin colour. Because of her religion.

Because of all the things that never mattered to him.

I just wish I wasn't so scared.

His fear was paralysing him, rooting him to the spot, forcing him to jitter in a manic, immobile state.

"Okay," he forced himself to whimper.

Taking it as her cue, Suniya pushed one of the dumpsters aside with her body, forcing a narrow gap. Surveying the area, she confirmed they were alone in the alley and she squeezed her way through the short escape from the messy stench they had hidden in.

Eric reluctantly followed.

He followed Suniya through the alley, stepping over the corpse left discarded upon the floor. He shut his eyes as tightly as he could to avoid gagging, forcing his eyelids together like weights.

When he opened them, he found his hand in Suniya's as she led him to the edge of the alley. After peering her head out, she flinched it back, pressing herself up against the wall, forcing Eric to do the same.

"What is it?" he gasped, shaking frantically.

"There's loads of them," she replied, her eyes fluttering as her wired mind whirred over possible solutions.

All that gumption he had manifested a short time ago had left his body like waste. Back then, it was fire and some bullies he was escaping.

And escaping was the correct word – he was running. Something he was very, very good at.

Running didn't take any courage whatsoever.

So that is what he had done.

Now, he was being made to face them. Not run, but to sneak past a whole mass of them who were waiting for blood.

On a second's prompt, he could run back into that alley, hiding once again. Taking Suniya with him.

He did not want to sneak past them.

He did not want to be caught.

"The door to the flat block is only yards away." Suniya turned to Eric, gazing sincerely into his eyes. "We can make it."

"No, we can't."

"We have to. They will come back into this alley at some point, Eric, there are too many of them. They've already executed one person here, how many more?"

"I know, I just—" Eric's eyes welled up. "I can't. I can't do it. I can't sneak past them."

"It's me they are after," Suniya growled. "If I can do it, so can you."

She turned her head and peered at the group of thugs guarding the pub beside them, more Molotov cocktails in their hands, ready to set whatever, or whomever, to a fiery death.

They were gathering in a circle, a man cowering beside their feet.

"They are distracted," Suniya turned her head back and told him.

Eric peered around, only allowing himself an inch, refusing to let himself risk being seen.

Sure enough, another Indian man had been caught and was laying on the floor, being tormented. The group of attackers who had killed another man not so long ago now gathered around another helpless soul. Throwing kicks, punches, blades; whatever they could into their helpless prey.

"It's now, Eric; they are distracted, we have to go."

Eric felt callous. Using the doomed fate of a poor, innocent man as their escape seemed inhuman.

But this wasn't about what was ethically right.

This was about surviving.

And he knew Suniya was right.

"On the count of three," she prompted him. "One."Eric peered across the street. More and more thugs had since gathered, each of them getting their kicks in, circling their victim with a salvo of assaults.

"Two."

Suniya shut her eyes, mentally preparing herself.

"Three."

Suniya ran forward, Eric's hand in hers. Eric went to go, then saw a man's head turn momentarily from beating the innocent man to their direction.

His hand slipped from Suniya's.

The next thing he knew, Suniya was standing beside the door to the flat block, what must have been only fifteen yards away, her eyes desperately reaching out to him.

Eric still stood in the alleyway.

She hovered outside the door.

She would be seen.

Eric could see that. She was visible to everyone.

Eric turned his head back to the man he thought he had glanced at them. The man now had his back to them, resuming his aggressive contributions to their circling attack.

"Eric!" Suniya pleaded to him, holding the door open, staring at the circling mob that could spot her any second.

She was waiting for him. In clear sight of anyone who turned and looked, she was waiting.

And still, he couldn't move.

A gunshot rang out.

The circle dispersed.

Another dead body lay on the floor.

The mass group now turned, resuming their previous positions, some of them meandering toward the flat block Suniya stood outside of.

Suniya still waited.

Tears flooded her cheeks.

Her arms shook in frenzied anxiety.

"Please, Eric," she mouthed.

With an abrupt leap forward, Eric stumbled to the ground.

Glancing over his shoulder as he lay on the floor of the street, he saw the mob picking up more lit bottles, turning to the other buildings of the street.

Turning toward them.

Pushing himself to his feet, he ran headfirst to Suniya, sprinting, his arms furiously waving with the accelerated motion of his legs.

Swinging the door open, he dove into the flat block, taking Suniya to the floor with him.

Eric looked out the glass window of the door, from the concealment of the shadows of the ground.

They were coming closer.

Suniya and Eric grabbed each other's hands and, without a moment's hesitation, ran to the staircase to begin their upward ascent.

CHAPTER TWENTY-SIX

A SCHOOL BUS.

What a joke.

If Jack was going to die, he was not going to die on a hijacked flipping school bus.

He surveyed the helpless faces around him. Some were police officers, with bruises and scars over tattered uniforms. Some were civilians, equally battered and beaten.

All avoided eye contact with him.

If only one of them would look at him, he could communicate. Plan something.

But, no.

None of them wanted to stand up, to fight, to see their way back to their families again.

What had these people done to them? How had so many police officers become so absently resolute?

Ridiculous question, really.

From what he had seen, the English Hearts were psychopathic arsonists. They had firebombed the police station, killing many great officers, and many good friends.

They had beaten him.

And even the army didn't have the courage to come in and take them on.

He had no idea how deep this thing had spread.

One of the men holding them hostage stepped forward, a large machine gun in his hand, a hood up and a scarf over his mouth so only his eyes were visible.

How the hell have they managed to get machine guns?

One, they could possibly buy. But to import this many, without getting caught or raising suspicion?

It means there had to be people higher up. They must have infiltrated many powerful people to put this operation together.

To create so much fear the army won't face them.

Another man with his machine gun over his back patrolled the corridor of the bus.

This man carried a toolkit in his hand.

This was an opportunity.

Jack fell to the floor, collapsing on top of the toolkit in the guy's hand and flailing about on the ground. The toolkit flew out of the guy's hand and spread over the floor. His hands were still painfully restrained and it hurt his wrists, but the pain was something he was just going to have to deal with.

Jack rolled onto his back, groaning in fake pain.

The man lifted Jack up by the throat and threw him onto his seat, planting a few heavy punches from his fat ring hand just for good measure.

Jack made eye contact with this man.

He was just a boy.

Feeling blood dripping from his nose, Jack stuck out his tongue and licked it, not breaking eye contact with this scumbag for a moment.

One of the other men shouted something and the bus came to a stop, causing the angry boy to cease his evil glare at Jack and resume whatever it was they were doing.

Jack felt the screwdriver in his hand. It had worked. Whilst floundering on the floor, he'd managed to steal it and conceal it. Now he clutched it tightly, pushing it up his sleeve.

They were marshalled off the bus one by one and made to drop to their knees beside a river.

Jack knew this place.

It was Trentham.

Such a beautiful, riverside location. Too beautiful to be marred with such ravenously evil exploits.

A fleeting memory met his mind, from only a mere month ago. He had taken Vanessa and Tallah for a lovely spring evening walk beside the river. The gardens were so lovely and peaceful, it made for a wonderful family occasion. The kind of situation and beauty that made you contemplate life.

Now, look at it.

Blood marked the grass beside him. Bodily remains floated on the surface of the water.

The rain ceased, but the wind continued to grow. The river beside him grew unsteady.

"We don't need 'em mate," one of the men said to another man carrying a large weapon, which Jack recognised as a Russian ShKAS gun; a gun capable of firing 3,000 rounds per minute. "Get rid of the cunts."

The gun-wielding assailant made his way over to a Chinese man on his knees, three people down from Jack.

The gunman pointed the end of his barrel against the back of the whimpering man.

A rapid succession of bullets rang out, leaving a piercing screech vibrating through Jack's ears.

The Chinese man lay dead on the floor.

"Please, please, don't," begged the man two across from Jack.

The shotgun sang once more and the begging stopped.

Jack took a frantic look around himself, at the crying

victims beside him, at the masses of disguised attackers filling the vicinity.

He fumbled the screwdriver in his hand.

It was still there.

But what would he do with it?

What could he do with it?

The man beside Jack didn't want to kneel and die. He jumped to his knees and ran.

But he didn't get far.

The machine gun belted a series of low notes and the corpse flew flat-out onto the ground.

The gun reached Jack's head.

Feeling it press against his cranium, only two thoughts crowded his mind.

Vanessa.

Tallah.

Without hesitating, Jack flung his body across the ground and into the river. The gun rang out, narrowly missing Jack's legs.

Plunging further and further into the water, he shoved the screwdriver into the lock of his handcuffs, then twisted and twisted and twisted.

Bullets trickled quickly through the water beside him.

They were shooting at him.

They were not letting him go.

The handcuffs weren't opening. The fucking handcuffs were not opening.

And he was sinking deeper and deeper.

He couldn't breathe. He gasped for oxygen that didn't come.

Another bullet flew dangerously close to his knee.

The screwdriver twisted and twisted.

Then it twisted one final twist.

His hands were liberated.

He needed air. It didn't matter if he risked being shot, he needed air, or he wouldn't survive.

Running on pure adrenaline, he surged to the surface, reaching his mouth above water and taking in as much air as he could.

A gunshot found him and he ducked below the water, only narrowly escaping its death-inducing strike.

With the biggest strokes he could muster, he found his way through the river, further and further away from the bullets continually streaming toward him.

CHAPTER TWENTY-SEVEN

Eric's legs were like lead.

Almost twenty floors up and the prospect of the looming stairs still to come filled him with dread.

He stopped and bent over, grasping his knees, furiously panting.

"We need to keep going," Suniya urged him.

He vigorously nodded, recognising the need to keep going. But somehow his legs were not connecting with his brain.

He peered over the banister towards the floor.

No one followed.

"We're fine, we're safe for now," he assured her.

"Please, Eric. Come on."

Closing his eyes and taking a huge, deep breath, he lunged himself forward.

He tried taking the stairs two steps at a time, seeing if a larger stride would make it easier. Never had he been more aware of how unfit he was. Never had he regretted not undertaking a gym membership.

Grabbing hold of the banister, he dragged himself up and up and up.

Watching Suniya's hijab blow in the wind of her speed, he wondered how she had managed to surpass him with such energy.

Willing another surge of adrenaline to meet his body, he continued to drag himself up by the banister, clutching onto it with both hands, using all his might to propel him.

Finally, the end was in sight.

Just two more floors.

Two more shitty floors.

Suniya reached the top before he did, reaching a door he presumed led them to the roof. She awaited him, taking him by his hand as he fell to the top step, forcing himself through.

As soon as they made it onto the roof, he collapsed in a heap on the floor, struggling for breath. He panicked for a fleeting moment, terrified he was going to pass out, such was his need for oxygen.

Eventually, his panting subsided.

His breath caught up with his aching body.

Looking up, he saw Suniya standing at the edge of the roof, peering downwards.

Dragging himself to his feet, he forced himself to her side, letting the door to the stairs shut behind him.

"What is it?" he moaned, in a far more agitated manner than he had intended.

Suniya instantly rose her hand into the air and shushed him.

Her head rotated, his wide eyes met hers, a bead of sweat trickling down her forehead.

"Listen," she gasped, barely audibly.

Eric listened.

A faint rumble resounded in the distance.

Gazing at Suniya, his mind reached for guesses as to what the rumbling could be. The rain had left and, although overcast, there was no sign of thunder, nor of lightning.

The roof beneath them vibrated, calmly seizing, shaking with a looming intensity.

Jeers grew in the distance, a menacing shout accompanying the rumble.

Eric's eyes peered past the nearby buildings, desperate to find the source of the noise.

But, once he found it, he wished his eyes hadn't been so eager.

A cloud of smoke rose from the dusty ground, growing into an eerie mess. Following this impending rise of grey and white, were voices meeting the aggression of the thumping feet. Raindrops on the roof quivered into a seething shake. A rabid crowd drew near.

Crowd was a far nicer term than the mob should be afforded.

Hooligans after hooligans, thugs after thugs. A sea of faces disguised by caps, hoods, and scarves. These criminals parted into houses, invading homes, and businesses. The horde that followed behind them carried on down the street, plaguing the next set of doors.

Out of these buildings, they dragged any people they took a dislike to onto the street. Women in burkas and hijabs, men with turbans, people of brown or black skin. Dragged by their collars, thrown by their throats, and flung to the harsh floor of the city.

Their blood stained the cement beneath their corpses. Their throats slit, guts ripped apart, and body parts decapitated helplessly from their limbs.

Women. Children. Men.

Teenagers barely old enough to understand the world before them lay on their knees, crying over their parents' vacant eyes.

Old ladies who had lived such long, varied lives, were murdered in seconds.

Mothers were dragged kicking and screaming away from their babies.

Savages ravaged the homes, looting for people, withdrawing anyone who did not meet their expectation of a white Britain.

And, as Eric and Suniya stood open-mouthed and closed-fisted, gawking at the painful destruction inflicted on the streets below, a sickening sense of foreboding descended upon them.

The horde grew closer.

The crowd had ransacked the various buildings leading up to theirs. Mass gangs had flooded into buildings and executed their victims on the streets and in their homes.

Smashed windows of nearby buildings were stained with speckled blood.

Mothers threw their children out of the window, throwing them to their only possible salvation, screaming as they were withdrawn back into their buildings and plunged to their demise.

The buildings nearby were done.

English Hearts grew ever closer.

Suniya took out her phone. Why hadn't she thought of this before now? But Eric could only watch as she discovered it to be as useless as he had discovered earlier, the same fatal image of the English Hearts logo stuck on her display.

No lights or street-lamps lit the drenched paving slabs below. The only source of light came from fires cast upon nearby mosques and immigrant-owned off licenses.

"What do we do?" Eric gasped.

Suniya didn't look at him.

He gazed at her, willed her to meet his eyes, unconsciously begging her to respond.

It was no good.

She was staring at the ground, where the maddening horde of thousands descended upon the buildings they stood atop of.

Streams of murderers made their way through the doors below.

Heavy feet met the ground floor of the building they stood upon.

It was too late.

They were trapped.

CHAPTER TWENTY-EIGHT

A SCREWDRIVER MAKES a resourceful weapon but requires strength behind it to ensure a lethal touch. Jack would need something new.

As he snuck across a barren road toward Hanley town centre, he came across a bridge that served as sufficient cover for him to pause. The river that gave him his escape now weighed heavily on his clothes. His drenched, tattered uniform clung to him with a weighty attachment.

It was not practical.

Shooting his eyes back and forth to confirm that he was alone – as alone as he could reliably be – he grappled his t-shirt and trousers off. As he twisted them, he rung heaves of water into a puddle, then wafted them in anticipation of a drying breeze.

Hearing faint footsteps, he grabbed his clothes and pinned himself against the wall. Watching intently at the far side of the bridge that leads to a roundabout he had driven across so many times – he peered for the source of the voices.

He didn't realise how tightly he was clutching the screwdriver in his hand.

In the distance, two men with balaclavas and extravagantly large knives passed and walked away.

Releasing a large sigh, Jack quickly put his trousers on and, pushing himself firmly against the wall, crept to the opening of the bridge and surveyed the area. Once he had decided it was clear, he redressed himself and continued his journey toward the town centre.

Can't stop.

Got to keep moving.

Got to get to Vanessa. Tallah.

Got to help the army get in.

I may well be the only police officer left in the city.

He neared the shops surrounding the outskirts of the town, creeping from building to building, his eyes always peering back and forth, back and forth, his attention never wavering.

As he approached the sound of voices, he flung himself behind the nearest building and cautiously peered out from behind it.

One. Two. Three. Four. Five.

Five men.

All armed with knives.

No, not knives.

Large, curved, sharp-bladed meat cleavers.

But they weren't trained. They didn't have a skillset. They stood like idiots, like people who had watched one too many movies. They didn't stand like trained killers or fighters.

Something that could be used to Jack's advantage.

He needed their weapons.

If he was to come across anyone who had a bit more to them, those weapons were essential.

So there he was.

Five on one.

Five meat cleavers against a screwdriver.

A sudden wave of anxiety consumed him. His distaste for

the unpleasant side of his job resurfaced. A few years ago, he would have had no problem engaging in a lethal battle.

But now...

Now he may have to take a life.

Could he do that?

One of the group lifted a radio to his mouth and spoke something Jack couldn't make out above the muffle of his scarf. He nodded to the others and waved at the man next to him, who walked ahead of him, down the street toward Jack.

This was Jack's opportunity.

Jack grabbed the man who had spoken on the radio and flung him into the alleyway. He grabbed the second man with him also, taking a handful of this man's hair and driving his head into the wall enough times to knock him out.

As the first man got back to his feet and went to shout out, Jack tightened the man's scarf around his mouth, stifling any sound. Hooking the guy's ankles and sending him to the ground, he landed his knee on the guy's head with enough gravity to knock him unconscious.

He lifted his screwdriver in the air.

They would regain consciousness soon.

He had no choice.

He had to do this.

But I can't.

"Fuck's sake, Jack."

He couldn't do it.

Cursing himself under his breath, he hurled to his feet and ran into the street. He marched toward the remaining three scumbags.

Lunging the screwdriver forward, he stuck it into the side of the closest man's chest, lifting it above his ribs.

Jack knew this wasn't enough to kill the man.

It would just cause him too much pain to fight.

The next man came at him waving his meat cleaver and Jack ducked.

This was it.

I need to take the lethal blow.

Psyching himself up, willing himself, urging himself, mentally pushing, coercing, beating himself, Jack told himself he had to do it.

No choice.

Him or Jack.

Him or his family.

His family needed him.

Jack needed to kill the man for them.

He ducked another strike and swung the screwdriver upwards, sailing it into the man's neck.

Except, he didn't.

He held it there. Poised. An inch away.

He cried out.

I can't do it.

A slash clawed down Jack's back and he fell to his knees.

The remaining three men surrounded him, weapons in the air.

CHAPTER TWENTY-NINE

THE FRAGILE WALLS of the flat block violently trembled. The nearby rumble turned to nearby screaming. The smashing of doors, the shrieks of terror, the charging of the attackers – chaos consumed the air.

Eric was sure they were safe on the roof. No one would look on the roof.

Surely.

As soon as that thought crossed Eric's mind, a woman burst onto the roof of the adjacent building. Drawn by the woman's horrific squealing at Eric and Suniya for help, they both hurried to the edge.

Could this woman jump?

If she were to leap onto their roof, could she make it?

Eric looked to Suniya, seeing in her eyes that she too was looking for a way to help this woman.

A man burst onto the roof, topless, with grey tracksuit trousers and a balaclava, proudly displaying the faded tattoo of a swastika upon his chest.

This woman screeched, turning toward them with eyes wide full of terror.

There was no escape for her.

The man brandished a machete. Grabbing the lady from behind, he plunged the machete through her back, thrusting it through her heart. She died instantly, turning to a puppet dangling on the end of his weapon.

As he allowed the body to slide the floor, his bloodshot eyes turned to those of Eric and Suniya.

There was no hesitation.

Eric and Suniya sprinted to the door, bursting back into the stairwell.

Thundering steps pounding against the metallic stairs reverberated around the hollow tube. Eric peered over the bannister. A quarter of the way up from the ground were hordes of ruthless, masked killers, barging against each other to get up the stairs first, thirsty for blood.

Suniya kicked the door to the top floor open and Eric followed.

What would they do now?

Where would they go?

Eric knew he should protect Suniya. He knew it was his duty, he loved her more than anything – but it became very apparent to his thoughts that it was not him they were after.

No. Please. For once in your life, Eric, do not be a coward.
You will not desert the woman you love.
She would not desert you.

He felt guilt for even entertaining the thought. But, be honest, even if it was only a fleeting option flying past your mind – would you not consider the same?

Suniya banged on door after door, squealing for help against each barrier.

The tirade of footsteps echoed closer and closer.

Eric was rooted to the spot.

He didn't see how any of these flats could conceal them, even if they found someone willing to help. Everyone in these flats would want to protect themselves and their family. In situations like this, true human nature revealed itself; no one would risk their own safety to help.

Why would they risk their life for a stranger?

The muffled voices grew audible.

"In here."

"Get the fuck out!"

"Paki scum gonna die!"

Eric's eyes watered.

Sudden flashes of Suniya's death engrained themselves on his thoughts.

What would he tell her parents?

Would they blame him?

Would they see him as the enemy?

Eric couldn't bear the thought of such a fate bestowing itself upon Suniya.

As she helplessly launched herself against the final few doors, he remained feebly paralysed. This wasn't him deserting her. This was him being realistic.

Or so he told himself.

As he watched her, he saw a machete plunged through her back.

He saw her throat squeezed shut as she squealed like Ahmad did.

She saw her body strung up in the streets.

So much pain to come. So much.

Maybe the humane thing to do would be to just end it for her?

As if.

As if Eric would ever have the guts.

The final door opened and a man revealed himself. A gentle-looking soul, with neatly parted hair and plain white skin. He looked like an honest, working man.

Whoever he was, he was the only one to offer refuge.

As Suniya threw herself into his flat, she waved at Eric to follow.

Glancing to his side, he saw shadows against the wall of the staircase growing bigger. The omen of death, a silhouette growing with the shouts of hate.

He ran forward, bouncing against the wall and into the flat.

The man locked the door just as they heard the beastly screams enter the floor.

CHAPTER THIRTY

Suniya collapsed in a weeping mess.

All the death, all the anxiety, all the desperate attempting to escape, flooded her body with a hectic weight, pulling her to the floor.

"Please, they will hear you," the man told her. "You have to get away from the door."

Suniya felt herself hoisted to her feet. She could tell it was Eric's arms; she could always tell when it was those arms. She rested herself against his chest as he took her to a sofa and sat her down.

Her breathing wheezed with a hoarse, croaky filter that stained her throat.

The floor was blurry. The colours melded together into a sinister combination of pixelated grey, black and red.

"Suniya, breathe," she heard Eric's voice.

His hands were on her knees. She could feel them.

But she couldn't think.

Images shot through her head, from frantic vision to frantic vision.

The machete cut through that woman's heart.

Ahmad executed.

People being pulled out of their homes, onto the streets, slaughtered.

People like her.

Muslims.

Muslims were being tortured and there was no one stopping it.

She could hear them in the corridor, hear them banging, hear screams of people being dragged, thumps against the wall, victorious yelps melded with begs and whimpers.

They were going to reach this flat eventually.

She was going to die.

She knew it.

How could they escape?

"Suniya, I need you to calm your breathing, I need you to focus."

She looked up.

Her blurred vision turned to hazy lines. She could make out Eric. He was on his knees in front of her. Staring avidly into her eyes. Taking her hands in his. Shaking them. Shaking her. Willing her. Talking.

Constantly talking.

"Suniya, we are not out of this yet, you need to be here with me. Come on."

Her hearing had returned,

Her breathing was quieter.

She was still panting, but her breaths weren't a resounding panic.

She coughed on invisible smoke and calmed her breathing down.

"I can hear them outside," she gasped.

"I know, I know, but it's okay," Eric reassured her. "This man is going to take care of us. His name is Craig."

His name was Craig?

When had Eric gotten this man's name?

Suniya turned her head and saw Craig standing, his arm around a woman she assumed was Craig's wife or girlfriend, his concerned eyes looking back.

"Can you help us?" Suniya asked.

"Hide in the bathroom. There is a closet in there. We will do our best to keep them away from you."

Suniya nodded.

She felt a weighty tug on her arm. Eric had pulled her to her feet and dragged her through a corridor. He shoved her into the bathroom and locked the door behind him.

"Don't lock the door," Suniya instructed, staring gormlessly at the handle.

"What? Why?" Eric grabbed hold of her arms and looked nonsensically into her eyes.

"Because then they'll know someone's in here."

She had no idea how she'd thought so clearly, but somehow, she had.

Spinning around, she twisted the tap and threw a sink full of water over her face. She lifted her eyes and looked in the mirror.

Her hazel eyes gazed back.

Her brown skin so clear. So beautiful. So wicked.

"Suniya, we need to hide in the cupboard," Eric instructed.

She turned and stared at him.

She couldn't move.

Something was wrong.

Something was really, really wrong.

"Suniya?"

"Shush."

Ignoring Eric's perplexed stare, she listened intently.

"We need to contact Bruno Tug," came a voice from outside the bathroom.

Suniya drifted carefully to the door and listened to the foggy murmurs.

"I'm telling you," came a woman's voice. "I should call him."

"No!" Craig snapped. "I let them in here, I got her. She will be a perfect candidate for the martyr. It's part of his plan. I know this. I should call him."

Suniya fell to her knees. Her legs could no longer support her.

"Oh my God." As soon as the words escaped her lips, she had no idea how they had managed to.

"Who is Bruno Tug?" Eric shot. "What is the martyr?"

Suniya knew who Bruno Tug was.

She knew exactly who he was.

CHAPTER THIRTY-ONE

"You really think she'd be the perfect candidate? For the martyr, I mean?"

"Of course. He said he wants a young woman, someone remotely attractive. She seems a divine choice."

"Shall I call him?"

"No, I will call him. I found her, I will call him."

"That's not fair!"

"Shut up, of course it is. Just think. How besotted will Bruno Tug be with me after I find him his perfect martyr?"

The well-spoken nature of Craig and his partner's voices severely contrasted with the crassness of their subject.

What were they planning to do?

Suniya could tell they were planning on giving her to the leader of English Hearts, Bruno Tug – that much was clear. But why were they calling her the martyr?

Don't martyrs die?

Suniya's eyes darted around the room, avidly searching for an escape.

There was nothing.

There was a tiny window at the top of the room barely wide

enough to fit a dog, never mind a fully-grown person. A shower, a toilet, a sink – nothing they could use as their route out, or even as a weapon.

Her breathing quickened. Her arms shook.

Claustrophobic. Trapped. Hunted.

Hunted like an animal to be slaughtered.

Three loud bangs resided against the front door of the flat.

"They're here!" came an excitable yelp from down the corridor.

"Quick, let them in!"

Suniya's eyes shot to Eric. "What are we going to do?"

Eric's eyes looked vacantly back at her. She could tell he was racking his thoughts for answers just as she was, but was coming up with nothing.

"We need to get out of this bathroom," Suniya decided. "We have no chance of escaping from here. There's a bedroom through the corridor."

"What if they see us?" was Eric's startled reply.

"We stand no chance in here!" Suniya barked.

The front door opened.

"We need to do it now, while they are at the front door, while they are distracted."

Suniya's wide, terrified eyes willed Eric to hurry up, get on board.

Aggressive cheers filled the entrance to the flat.

"Come on," Suniya demanded, not waiting a moment longer.

Placing her hand delicately on the door handle, she opened it with the slightest of nudges. Through the gap in the door she peered down the corridor, trying to make out what was going on.

Through the corner of the twist of the hallway, she could make out numerous voices and could see numerous shadows.

One.

Two.

Three.

Four.

There were four. At least.

Plus Craig and his partner; that was six against two.

Staying there any longer would mean certain death.

However much the odds were piled against her, she had to do it. She had to find some way.

She had to.

Brushing away a stray tear, she carefully opened the door, slow enough to quell its squeak. She led Eric into the hallway, peering at the distant assailants greeting each other with dubious joy.

Pinning herself against the hallway wall, Suniya placed the slightest of steps against the floor, one after each other, slowly, precisely, warily.

The bedroom door. It grew closer.

She listened. The greetings had ended. Footsteps thumped against the mangled carpet.

No more time for stealth.

She picked up her pace and threw herself into the bedroom, grabbing Eric in with her, and shut the door with urgent fragility.

"They are in here," came Craig's hushed voice, followed by a rat-a-tat-tat against the bathroom door.

"Guys, could you just come out a minute?" his voice softly enquired.

Suniya's panicked eyes nervously darted around the room. Her eyeline burst to every various corner and crack, taking in everything.

A double bed. A wardrobe. A double glass door leading to a narrow porch.

Could they hide in the wardrobe?

Or under the bed?

But what then?

Once they had run out of places to search, they would find her. Eric wouldn't have the strength to protect her, and she wouldn't have the strength to protect herself; together they couldn't fight six people.

What then?

"Guys, please open the door." Craig's voice grew increasingly impatient.

Across the room was a double door made of glass; Suniya rushed to it and peered out.

They were at least thirty floors up. The porch was around a metre in width, not even big enough for them to fit on together; and even if they did, there was no way they could jump to their escape and survive.

But there was a building opposite.

How far away was it?

Could they jump?

She could make out rows of porches, about the same size, below all the windows in the opposite building. Even if they didn't reach the one directly opposite, then they could hopefully grab onto one below as they fell.

But what if they didn't manage to grab onto it?

How far was it?

Too far. You could fit another building in that space. It was too far. Way too far.

But the alternative was get killed, right there, in that flat.

"Guys, we are coming in," Craig's agitated voice declared. There was a barge against a door, into what Suniya knew would turn out to be an empty bathroom.

"Where the fuck are they?" came an angry voice that was not Craig's, and was far more menacing.

Suniya tried the porch door. It was locked.

Her eyes shot to Eric.

Footsteps stomped against the ground, growing quickly closer.

It was now or never.

"Eric." She grabbed onto his arm. "I need you to smash this window."

CHAPTER THIRTY-TWO

THERE WAS NO CHOICE.

Jack was going to have to kill them.

It was him or them. His survival or their survival.

If he died, he would never be able to get back to his family; he would never be able to contact the outside.

So many lives depended on him living.

He had to live.

It was kill or be killed.

But how could he face himself? How would his family face him? How could he go on, forever seeing blood on his hands?

The man he had settled a screwdriver into the side of found his feet. Clutching onto the side of his chest, blood soaking through his t-shirt, he staggered forward. He stood beside his comrades, unanimously snarling at their prey with their meat cleavers raised.

I'm going to have to do this.

Willing tears away from his eyes, willing the thought of his daughter, the father he was, the kind of man he was – pushing it all into the depths of his mind, he stood forward. His hand gripped the screwdriver so hard it hurt his bones.

This was it.

One of the men leapt forward, launching his cleaver backward in preparation, readying a foul, swift swipe.

Jack fell to his knees and ducked the swipe, jamming his screwdriver into the man's legs, then withdrawing it and flying his hand upwards.

Flying his hand to the man's throat.

Sticking the screwdriver in.

The man gurgled, blood trickling down his jaw.

Jack punched the screwdriver, forcing it further in, putting his weight behind a swift, heavy action that plunged the utensil into the man's windpipe.

Jack snatched the meat cleaver from the man's hand, clutched onto it, and slit the guy's throat as he fell to the floor.

That was the strangest part.

Using the weapon of a racist murderer.

Somehow, using their weapon made him feel far guiltier. Like it was worse than using the screwdriver. Like it made him as bad as they were.

Turning around, Jack steadied his eyes upon the two attackers facing him.

The two Jack had previously disarmed in the alley fumbled their way to their feet and joined them. Bloody bruises spread over the forehead of the man whose head Jack had rammed into the wall, and a bleeding nose from the other whose face had harshly met Jack's knee.

Four lethal blows.

That was the barrier between Jack and survival.

Four men ready to kill him.

The man still grasping his bloody ribs jumped forward with an evil growl, desperate for revenge, and stumbled onto his hands. It didn't take much for Jack to apply the fatal touch to that man's throat.

The remaining assailant who had yet to be harmed by Jack charged forward, followed by the remaining two.

Taking the weapon off the man Jack had only just dispatched, he raised the two grand weapons into the air and buried them into the chests of the two charging at him.

One left.

The man turned on his heel and limped away, stumbling dizzily. To this man, he must be sprinting – but to Jack, the man was barely plodding forward, knocking himself off each wall in turn.

The man was not attacking Jack. He was running away.

Jack could let him go.

Surely.

Surely that's a life he needn't take?

No.

Jack knew the truth.

If this man was to escape and was to meet up with any other members of the English Hearts descending their reign of terror upon the city, he would recall Jack's presence. Tell of Jack's attack.

Jack couldn't risk that.

As much as he wished he could, he couldn't.

Not if he was to contact the outside. No one could know he was alive.

Sighing with reluctance, a hefty breath exuding the struggles of a heavy mind, he lurched himself forward.

After a few long strides, he caught up with the man.

Jack kicked the man's feet out from beneath him and stood over him. With only the man's bruised forehead showing, Jack ripped away the scarf concealing the person's identity and stifled a horrified gasp.

It was a teenager. A child. Barely old enough to be a man.

Some scummy kid who had been poorly raised, crying like a baby.

"Please..." the teenager begged. "Please, don't hurt me..."

"How old are you?" barked Jack.

"Eighteen... I just turned eighteen..."

Jack bowed his head. How could he do this? Kill an unarmed eighteen-year-old?

He reminded himself that this boy had made his choice. He was old enough to fight in a war, he was old enough to be responsible for his own actions.

Jack wished there was a way he could help him. Normally, he would. He would arrest him and find him a program, find some way to keep him off the streets, give him some help.

But there was a bigger picture.

There was his survival. His family's survival. The city's survival, if he could help in the way he thought he might be able to.

One boy who could give it all away. Was it worth the risk?

I wish it was.

"Please..." the boy pleaded.

"I'm sorry."

With a swift, foul swipe, the boy's blood splattered across the pavement and his suffocation was brief.

Jack fell to his knees.

Tears trickled down his cheeks. His hands grabbed his hair, pulled it out, clenched tightly into furious fists.

He let out a scream. He knew it was stupid, someone could hear him, someone could find him by following the voice.

But Jack didn't care.

Jack had never wanted to hurt anyone.

Jack had never wanted to be made a monster.

I need to move. I need to find cover. If they find me here, surrounded by dead bodies of their own...

He knew what he had to do, but his body wouldn't move. He was paralysed. Fixed in a static motion of severe, unfaltering, indefatigable grief.

Come on. Move.

His eyes fell upon the stationary eyes of the boy staring back at him.

Pushing his hands against the ground, forcing himself up, he dragged himself away. Grabbing a radio from one of the nearby bodies and tucking the two meat cleavers into the back of his trousers, he crept to his next building for cover.

In the reflection of the building's windows, the boy's eyes gazed back at him.

CHAPTER THIRTY-THREE

Eric grabbed the pristine, white bed sheets, and ripped them apart until he had a large strip of cloth. Glancing over his shoulder at the doorway, the only separation between commotion in the hallway and them, he wrapped the bed sheets over his knuckles.

"Come on, Eric!" Suniya cried, her eyes adamantly fixed upon the bedroom door. The handle shook under the heavy footsteps of the agitated assailants marching through the hallway.

"Where the fuck is she?" an angry northern voice growled.

"She was in here!" cried Craig. "She must be somewhere."

Eric rushed to the glass doors and retracted his hand. Putting all his strength and speed into his swing, he threw his fist forward and into the glass.

Pain shot like a rapid lightning bolt up his fingers and through his arm.

Falling to the floor, he grabbed hold of his wrist, clutching his hand, moaning in agony.

The glass remained intact.

"Come on, Eric," Suniya urged.

"It hurts…"

"Just go through it, Eric, please, you have to, please!"

Booming footsteps paraded down the corridor. Photo frames of happy memories and items of holidays gone shook with the furniture they stood upon. The heavy stomping grew closer, and Suniya kept her stare glued to the door in anticipation.

"Try the bedroom," growled a voice.

"*Eric!*" Suniya screamed.

"I heard her! She's in the bedroom!"

Shit.

Eric sprang to his feet.

Got to keep going.

Ignore the pain. Ignore it, and power through. The pain is temporary, it's fleeting. Endure the pain and keep their lives. Simple trade.

He struck his fist against the glass once more.

Agony shot up his arm, jarring his knuckles, his bones weak.

"Fuck!" he gasped.

The door to the bedroom slammed open and the heavy black boots of a masked, muscular man filled the frame.

"Eric…"

Eric lifted his arm back and struck again.

And again.

And again.

A crack appeared.

The man charged forward, followed by numerous other men, followed by Craig.

Two more strikes.

The window smashed.

"Go!" Eric cried out.

Suniya narrowly missed the reaching claw of the well-built attacker. Pushing forward, away from his clutches, she dove onto the porch.

Gulping down her fear, she perched on the wooden beam and used it to project herself forward.

Eric choked on a quick intake of oxygen.

He watched with bated breath and mouth wide open as Suniya's arms and legs dangled through the air. Flailing out, she made it half-way down the opposite building, grabbing onto the wooden beam of a porch at least ten floors down. Her legs swung back and forth until she eventually gained control and struggled herself over the wooden beam, and onto the porch.

Eric released his stifled breath.

Then he remembered. He wasn't alone.

Suniya peered up to Eric with despairing eyes, gesturing for him to follow.

Glancing over his shoulder, he saw an angry snarl wipe over the man's face.

Eric turned on his heel and ran to the porch, readying himself, about to jump, knowing what he needed to do; just jump, just get it done.

Simple.

Suniya did it.

As soon as he got to the porch and leant half over the wooden beam, he lost his breath and froze.

People on the floor were like ants. Tiny, angry men, busily rushing. Minute.

If he hit the floor he'd surely die.

Too late. A huge fist grabbed the back of his collar and flung him back into the room. The last thing he saw was Suniya. Suniya bouncing on the spot with desperate urging. Terrified tears and waving arms.

Eric was thrown onto the floor so hard he felt his face convulse as it hit the floor. He turned himself over. A huge, fat fist landed into his eye. He clutched it, feeling it throb.

The man took Eric by the throat, lifting him up and pinning him against the wall.

Eric fought for breath. His arms thrashed out at the man, peeling at his face, hitting his arm. It was no good. The man was too strong.

A quick glance to his side showed him Craig's worried face. Craig looked back at Eric with wounded eyes.

Craig. The coward.

The man who gave them refuge, whom they trusted, and ended up betraying that trust.

Was this man like Eric? Taking the easy way out. Doing whatever he had to, to survive, despite however immoral it was?

If Craig had to jump to the adjacent building, would he back out too?

Probably.

Craig wasn't that different. Eric was only one mistake away from being him.

And Eric did not want that to be his final thought.

He swung his leg back and launched it between his assailant's shin and lower knee.

Taking his attacker's howl of pain as his opportunity, he hit the guy's elbow and dropped to the floor.

It was now or never.

Eric sprinted forward, rushing to the porch, jumping onto the beam.

Not looking down.

Not thinking about the men reeling behind him. Chasing him. Hungry for his blood.

He jumped.

Seeing Suniya's arms reaching out for him, he reached back.

But he missed.

Her sorrowful eyes disappeared from view as Eric fell further down.

In a moment of respite, he managed to only just scrape the porch below the one Suniya occupied.

His grip didn't last. The beam was wet and slippery, and just as he felt a wave of relief, his hands let go.

He fell the few floors to the ground, landing on his back with a painful groan.

The chaos of the mob ran past him, pulling people out of buildings, continuing to torture them.

Pulling Muslims out of the building next to his groaning body.

The building where Suniya hid, alone.

STAFFORDSHIRE TIMES

TERRORISTS IN OUR OWN COUNTRY

The prime minister was called back from his holiday this morning, to devastating news of a city under siege.

In his press conference, he said, "These people are animals. I wish to assure anyone of any culture living in Britain – these people do not represent us. They are disgusting, abhorrent creatures, who will be dealt with firmly by the law."

Despite the claims that the law will deal with these tyrants, there appears to be no action. The army and reinforcements from police all around the country have reached the city's border, but have gone no further. The border seems to be the limit.

Hovering by the edge, they seem too scared to go in. We are not sure why, but this is a disturbing development.

Stoke-on-Trent, our thoughts are with you.

CHAPTER THIRTY-FOUR

THE MOON HUNG at the highest point of the sky, casting black shadows over a city stained with red. Grey clouds hovered carelessly overhead and the smell of fine rain filled the air.

Jack crept forward, keeping himself low, his hand clutched to the weapon tucked into the back of his trousers.

The darkness of the night, mixed with the anxiety afflicting his mind, made it difficult for him to keep his bearings. He was aware that he was approaching Hanley town centre, but was unsure of his precise location.

A street sign reflected the dim light of the moon. Never had the absence of street-lamps been more obvious.

Trinity Street.

Jack knew where he was.

Just around the corner from the Potteries Shopping Centre.

A voice.

Jack abruptly ducked into the doorway of a nearby building, peering around the corner at the street ahead.

"Reporting back to base," a man spoke into his radio as he heaved past, a heavy machine gun held high in his hand.

Base?

Potteries. The shopping centre.

They were using it as their base. As their hive.

This was good.

It gave the army a target.

Jack took the radio he'd stolen from his back pocket, turned it on and lifted it to his ear, taking in the various voices.

"Bruno wants the martyr candidate now."

"Where's he doing it?"

"Base."

"The Potteries."

"Safe."

"Mate, we can't find a fuckin' martyr, we killed every bitch we found."

"Some guy called Craig found one. They are just searching her out now."

"Can't wait."

"Fuck yeah, I'm on my way back to base. Can't wait."

"Bitch is gon' get burnt."

No more.

Jack could listen to no more.

He twisted the frequency of the radio, sifting through the static.

He took it to 169.325 MHz.

The police frequency for Staffordshire.

He listened.

There was nothing.

In all honesty, Jack wasn't entirely sure what he was expecting. Maybe just someone asking for help, some hope, some remnants of police lives still begging for help.

But there was nothing.

He couldn't broadcast on this frequency. These guys were efficient and organised, they would know what the police frequency was.

But there was that one time when he was in his twenties. A

brief period he was undercover. He had a secret frequency to broadcast on.

I wonder...

Turning to 172.988 MHz, Jack listened.

"Hello?" he tried.

The static ceased.

But no one answered.

It was over fifteen years ago, they would have changed it. It was a foolish idea.

"Hello?" came a voice in reply. It was a child's voice. Most likely a toddler.

"Hello, who is this?"

"It's Mikey, who is this?"

Jack sighed a huge sigh of relief.

He had contact. With a child, yes, but it was a start.

What if they were checking this frequency? What if they were listening in?

Too late now. It was his only shot.

"Hi, Mikey, my name is–" Jack stopped. If they were listening, he couldn't give his real name "–a friend. Can I speak to your daddy?"

"Why do you want to speak to my daddy?"

"Please, Mikey, I need you to do me this huge favour. Get me your daddy."

"Daddy!" the boy shouted out.

After a few moments, a disgruntled voice came through the radio.

"Hello? Who is this?"

"Hello, please, please, listen carefully. I am a police officer. I am currently trapped in Stoke-on-Trent."

"Stoke?" the man's shocked voice replied. News about the city's state had evidently gotten out.

"Yes, listen, I need you to phone 999. Then I need you to

give them this frequency. 172.988 MHz. I need you to do this now, please."

"I'm right on it." A few moments and the man's faint voice was heard. "Hello? Yeah, I got this guy on the radio, he says he's in Stoke-on-Trent, he gave me this frequency, he sounds pretty stressed."

The man returned to the radio.

"They say they are going to contact you now."

"Thank you so much."

A few seconds passed, and a far more professional voice spoke through the radio.

"Hello, this is Inspector Lewis David of the West Midlands Police. Can I ask who I'm speaking to?"

Jack's huge sigh of relief briefly relaxed his body, but it only took seconds for his shoulders to grow tense again.

"I can't give you my name, I don't know who's speaking. But I am a police constable in Staffordshire, I am in Hanley, in the attacked city."

"How many police officers are with you?"

Jack bowed his head.

"None. No one survived. I am the only officer."

The moment of silence made clear to Jack their disappointment.

"How can we be sure this is real?" responded the voice.

Jack thought. It was a good question. If they were going to trust him, he needed to trust them.

"My name is Jack Taylor. My distress code is zero nine eight."

He waited a few seconds for them to check.

"Well, we are pleased you could respond to us, Constable."

"What do I do?"

"We need to get into the city. We have an entry point, only it's not that simple. We could do with some help getting through."

"Okay."

"But if we can't be sure if anyone's listening…"

"We don't really have much choice."

"I guess you're right, Jack. Looks like you're our man. We're going to give you details of the location, and we need you there in an hour. Is this doable?"

"On one condition."

"And what condition is that, Jack?"

Jack ran a hand through his hair, surprised by how sweaty he was.

"Before you come into the city, you withdraw my family first. My wife and my daughter."

"We can't risk taking anyone out, Jack; otherwise we will give away us coming in."

"Those are my conditions. It's that or nothing."

The man hesitated.

"Okay, Jack. Okay."

CHAPTER THIRTY-FIVE

His bullish footsteps trod heavily against the hard, white floor. Leaning against the glass banister, he gazed downwards. What was once a clean, functional shopping centre, was now a building of burnt-out shops and flickering flames.

Bruno's sadistic smile grew as he feasted his eyes upon the anarchy.

Two of his men dragged another man, stripped down and screaming, along the floor. Behind them were four men with machine guns pointed at the captive's head.

The captive didn't struggle. Instead, he pleaded. Begged for mercy. Reached out for forgiveness Bruno had no intention of giving.

They brought the man up the dead escalators and threw him at Bruno's feet. Immediately, the man looked up at the leader, quivering shamefully.

"Please, please, it was not my fault, please don't hurt me," the man rattled on.

"Shut up," Bruno instructed, withdrawing a machete and cleaning it with his handkerchief.

"Please, please, I didn't mean it, it wasn't my fault—"

"*Shut. Up.*"

Bruno's loud, aggressive, hostile words reverberated against the walls of the potteries.

Once Bruno had thoroughly concluded his machete was clean, he placed his handkerchief back in his pocket. The weapon hung loosely by his side as he crouched before the man.

"Please…" he whispered, violently shaking.

"What is your name?"

"Tristan."

"Okay, Tristan. You were given an instruction. Can you tell me what it was?"

"Please, please don't hurt me."

"What was your instruction?!"

Tristan sobbed pathetically, covering his head with his hands, scrunching his face like a petulant toddler.

"You told me to kill the remaining police officers."

"And what happened?"

"One got away."

"One got away!" Bruno echoed, then continued with a small, ominous, quiet voice. "And a nigger officer, no less?"

Tristan nodded his head with furious tears.

"I've learnt something else about you too, Tristan. About your parents."

"My parents have nothing to do with this!"

"Your mother, your sweet, sweet, mother. Was a browny."

"Please, my mother has nothing to do with this."

"Is that not right?"

"My mother had brown skin, yes, but she wasn't Muslim, wasn't foreign, she wasn't like them –"

"*They are all like them!*"

In a strike of rage, Bruno plummeted his machete downwards and sank it into Tristan's folded leg, then retracted it almost as quickly. Tristan cried out in pain whilst desperately applying pressure, blood trickling through his fingers.

"Do you know what I think?" Bruno bellowed, pacing back and forth. The generals of the English Hearts stood at the edge of every surrounding floor, eagerly watching on. "I think you like them!"

Bruno used a handkerchief to wipe the blood from his machete. Once done, he tucked the machete into the back of his belt and folded his arms.

"Please, please don't stab me again..." Tristan muttered.

Bruno crouched down beside him.

"What was that?"

"Please don't stab me again..."

"Don't stab you again?"

"No..."

"Okay."

Tristan looked up in hope.

Bruno lifted him over the glass bannister and sent him plummeting to the bottom floor of the shopping centre.

A cracking snap accompanied Tristan's landing, his neck breaking against the marble floor.

Bruno turned to the general who had brought Tristan to him.

"Where is my martyr?" he demanded.

"We found the perfect girl. Young. Pretty... for one of them. A fighter."

"Do you have her?"

"A source told us had her. But she escaped."

"Well then, where is she?"

"They are still trying to get her now. She won't have gone far."

Bruno's fists clenched into a burning grasp of rage.

"Get Pearson on it," he demanded, his voice deliberate and menacing.

Bruno hmphed and stormed away. He strode across the shopping centre until he reached the prepared effigy he had demanded to be created.

He stopped suddenly, in awe at its beauty.

A large wooden stake had been erected in the middle of the shopping centre, logs around it, piled up, ready to make a fire.

Ready to burn.

The rope was already around the centre of the stake, ready to fasten to the girl.

The martyr.

CHAPTER THIRTY-SIX

Suniya didn't realise how much her hands were hurting. She gripped the bannister so tightly, putting all her stress, worry, and terror into her hands.

On the street below her, Eric was stirring, clambering to his feet, wearily looking around.

"Eric!" Suniya cried out.

Eric looked up. Saw Suniya. His eyes fell. Worry seeped across his face.

"Suniya?"

A violent noise lashed out and diverted Suniya's attention. Eric was tucked into a small street between the two buildings, but across from him, in the main street, chaos loomed.

Roars hung in the air like smoke. Masked men bombarded the doors below, pouring into her building, clad in scarves and caps and balaclavas, full of triumphant screams of hatred.

They held their weapons high above their head as they howled their war cry. Guns. Knives. Machetes. Meat cleavers. Cricket bats.

Once again, she was trapped. Trapped with nowhere to go.

"Eric, please!" Suniya cried out once more.

"It's okay, Suniya," Eric answered. "I'll come in and meet you."

Eric rushed out of the alleyway. By the time Suniya had screamed at him that it wasn't safe, he was gone.

She was alone.

Turning around, she peered inside the room behind her, concealed by glass doors. She seized the handle and, to her surprise, the door flung open.

Her relief was short-lived. She choked as she saw sprays of blood scattered across the walls like a splattering of paint. A soft pool of dark-red gunk lay on the floor below the door handle, splashes of red dropping from the stained door, collapsing into a puddle.

Suniya stepped inside, twisting her head back and forth, constantly vigilant, constantly listening.

Silence.

Eerie, uncomfortable, deafening silence.

Tiptoeing forward, she made her way through a bedroom and peered into the corridor. Allowing her cautious feet to edge out, she plastered herself against the wall, creeping along, continually heeding the sickening silence.

She made it to the front door.

What was she going to do?

Maybe if she stayed there, she'd be safe? This flat had evidently already been put under strife. If these assailants thought that they'd already ransacked this flat, maybe she'd be safe.

Turning to the room next to her, she opened the door in search of a place to hide.

A nauseating thud combatted her ears and the stench of decay consumed the room. Beside Suniya's feet a hand fell, flickering droplets of blood against her trainers.

Suniya jumped back, hands over her gaping mouth.

The body of a woman stared up at her, a giant open wound

parted along her neck, and various lacerations made to her torso.

Suniya bolted to the front door, opened it, and unknowingly slammed it behind her.

As her panting lessened pace, voices around the corner of the corridor wandered across the vacant wind.

"You think you're a fuckin' British man, do ya?"

"You fuckin' mug, you ain't nothin'."

They were there. Along the corridor. Barely steps from where she was.

She pressed down against the handle of the flat she had just escaped from, seeking it once more for restitution, her safety from these potential murderous captors.

But the flat was locked.

It had automatically locked behind her.

Suniya scrunched her eyes and wept. Her body convulsed with tears.

"I'm goin' a break your fuckin' fingers off," the voices continued.

The corridor in the opposite direction led to a sudden dead end. The only way out was back through the locked door or along the corridor where the voices lay.

I'm going to die.

In a moment of desperate clarity, it struck her. An incontestably honest truth.

"You dirty Islamic scum."

They were going to find her.

And they were going to kill her.

Was there any way past them?

Maybe?

She knew it was improbable. Just her outright denial. How could she sneak past in a corridor that thin?

"See this? This is my knife."

Maybe she should kill herself, somehow. If these people

were going to torture her, it would be quicker for her to do it herself. A more desirable death. An escape from what would inevitably happen.

No.

Stop it, Suniya.

She needed to keep going. See if there was a way. If there was only a small chance there was a way to survive, she would need to take it. For her family. For her parents.

For Eric.

She crept along the corridor, reached the corner, and poked her eyes subtly around, ever so slightly, so she only just caught a glimpse of what was happening.

Two masked assailants had a young man pressed up against the wall, a timid victim of similar ethnicity to her.

As one of the attackers held a knife up to the throat of their victim, the other kept him pinned against the wall. The knife-wielding attacker removed his facial disguise. His features were prominent; a large nose and piercing eyes.

A large scar crept along half of his face, starting at his lower cheek, travelling past his eyebrow and onto his forehead.

The scar was an unsettling sight that sent shivers running up and down Suniya's spine.

"What's your name?" the scarred man demanded.

"Hamas," the man wept.

"Hamas? Dirty fuckin' Muslim name. You know what I'm gon' do to you, Hamas? You know what you deserve?"

"Please..."

The man stuck his knife into Hamas' gut, twisting it before releasing it. Hamas' screams of agony forced Suniya to cover her ears.

She ducked behind the wall, worried her gaping and sounds of repulsion would get her discovered. She had seen so much death already. She couldn't see any more.

But she needed to figure a way out. She needed to.

Peering around the corridor once more, she took the sight of Hamas' numerous further stab wounds and a groggy, dazed look on his face.

Across the corridor was her respite. Could she run for it? Creep past them?

It was too risky.

The masked man received a radio message and relayed it to the scarred man.

"Mate, apparently, the girl Bruno wants for the martyr is in this building. Finish him, man, come on. Imagine if we were the ones to bring her to him."

"You serious?"

"Yes, mate."

The scarred man grinned. He thrust the knife into Hamas' neck and dropped the suffocating body to the floor.

"Let's find her then."

Suniya watched Hamas die.

Then a flicker of hope caught her eye.

Across the corridor, peering around the far corner.

It was Eric.

Eric was here.

But the momentary respite was short-lived. Her breath caught in her throat, as the scarred man turned and walked in her direction.

CHAPTER THIRTY-SEVEN

Eric wished he was brave.

If he was brave, he would have jumped out and fought those men as they turned toward Suniya.

If he was brave, he would have cried out to the woman he loved to run.

If he was brave, he would have revealed himself and offered his position as a distraction, so that the best thing that's ever happened to him could attempt to run.

As it was, he did none of those things.

He just watched.

Peered around the corner as Suniya's eyes reached out to him for help.

He stared at the body of Hamas. The body of a man rendered lifeless, a throat still bleeding lively. The body of a man who had been bestowed the fate he would likely be given should he try to be a hero.

He wanted to do something so much.

He urged himself to. Willed himself to be strong. To sacrifice himself for her. To throw some punches.

As it was, he was terrified of throwing punches. Terrified of getting hurt in any way.

Terrified of dying.

Expecting to break like glass at the slightest inclination of conflict.

He watched, feeling tears edge down his cheek. He held them back as best he could, as his sobs could give away his position.

The scarred man and his accomplice turned and walked toward Suniya. Suniya's eyes, that had only just made despairing contact with his, disappeared around the corner.

The two men followed Suniya around this corner.

Eric did nothing. He stood there, crying, praying she was okay, praying she would escape, that there was some way for her to get away.

But his legs were immovable. He willed them, told them to hurry, scolded himself for being so still.

Come on, Eric. Fucking run. Fucking jump out and help her. That's the woman you love, for fuck's sake!

But his thoughts did nothing to his legs. They stayed rooted like heavyweights wading through water.

A scream rang out down the corridor. A scream Eric uncontestably knew was Suniya. The definition of her voice was etched over her cry for help.

Her scream continued, turning to howls of pain.

That's when she said his name.

"Eric! Eric, please help me!"

Eric closed his eyes and bowed his head.

He wished he could do something. He wished he could see what was going on, that he could fight them and free her.

But he couldn't.

The next thing he knew, her screams were coming closer. He ducked behind a corridor, out of sight.

A scraping grew stronger, an indefinable drag across the floor.

The aggressive voices grew louder.

"You are a fuckin' pretty one, ain't ya?"

"Can see why he chose you."

"I'd fuckin' 'ave a go an' all."

"Maybe we should. We 'ave a bit of waiting time."

Watching from his concealed hiding place, Eric stifled his breath, keeping any sound hidden. The two men walked forward with their hands dug into Suniya's arms as they dragged her behind them.

Suniya saw Eric.

She reached out for him.

"Eric!" she cried.

Her face was bruised. Blood soaked half her top, and flickers of red stained her hijab. She was unable to struggle, too frozen with fear and pain to move out of their grasp.

But her eyes reached out to Eric. An inch of hope hurled out to him as she glanced over his face, thinking that maybe he was there to help. A moment of "thank God, Eric's here!"

But that moment went.

Eric pressed himself against the wall and remained silent so as not to be noticed.

Suniya's eyes fell.

Her hope drained.

The last thing Eric saw in her eyes before she disappeared around the corner was that despondent look. That terrified look of realisation as it dawned on her that the man she loved was going to do nothing to save her.

You're such a coward, Eric.

It was true.

But it gave him no comfort.

He could keep telling himself how gutless he was again and again, as if it was some feeble justification to his actions.

As if it made it okay.

It wasn't okay.

He was in love with her. Desperately, hopelessly in love with her.

And he had let her go. Let her be taken.

And done nothing.

And she knew that. The final sight she would have seen of him was that of him standing there helplessly. Refusing to do anything to save her. Refusing to intervene.

He fell to his knees.

He wept uncontrollably, despairing, seeping tears like bullets out of his eyes.

But it did nothing.

His tears did nothing.

What, they were supposed to make it okay? His being upset was supposed to excuse him from letting her be taken?

No.

No matter how much he cried, how much he admitted he was a coward, no matter how much he knew he was a piece-of-shit poor excuse for a man, it did nothing.

He had let her go.

CHAPTER THIRTY-EIGHT

Nearly there.

Nearly home.

Is Vanessa okay? Is she unharmed? Has anyone tried to hurt her?

Is Tallah safe?

These thoughts fought each other, crushing Jack's mind as he crept through the city. He cloaked himself in various shadows, always alert, always listening.

He'd grown accustomed to the smell of smoke. He barely went a minute without coming across another building licking itself with flames. The bodies that crossed his path were equally destructive to his fragile state of mind, and he did everything he could to not look at them – as every time he peered at another sickening corpse for too long, he saw Vanessa's helpless face in them.

Jack gagged as he turned down the next street, flinching at the sight of bodies strung up and left as a decoration of the hostile city.

Girls were roped around broken lamp-posts, their slit throats spewing dried blood beneath their flopped heads. All along the street, bodies were hung up and displayed like proud warnings.

Who would do this? What kind of people would see this as okay?

Turning past another flat block, he stepped over further various bodies of people beaten and left for dead. As he edged past an alleyway, he spotted a young man crying.

A white man. With glasses, a skinny body and evidently sensitive demeanour.

It could be a trap.

The man abruptly looked up, sensing that he was being stared at.

Jack clutched onto the meat cleaver wedged behind his belt, holding it, ready, his wide eyes fixed on this man.

Waiting. Prepared. Anticipating whatever this man was going to do.

The man did nothing. He dropped his hands from his weeping face and helplessly peered up at Jack.

"Please help me," the man whimpered, barely audible.

"Who are you?" Jack demanded, fierce aggression worn tightly upon his face.

"My name is Eric."

"You're white, Eric," Jack pointed out. "They are only killing minorities. You don't trick me."

"You don't understand..." Eric sobbed. "They took my girlfriend. She's a Muslim. They have her. I tried to protect her..."

Eric stopped himself and shook his head.

"No, I didn't. I let her go," he told Jack sincerely, a face full of longing regret. "They took her, and I let them."

Jack trusted him. This man couldn't be one of them. These attackers weren't waiting and tricking anyone, they were going out, full force, like racist Spartans in a violent battle. This was a weak, scrawny, childish man, full of fear.

Still, Jack wasn't going to take any chances.

"Stand up," Jack demanded.

"What?" Eric muttered meekly.

"Stand. Up."

Eric complied. Jack bustled up behind him and shoved him against the wall. Keeping one hand on his weapon, he used the other to pat Eric down. Once he was sure Eric was unarmed, Jack stood back and let his hands hang by his side.

Jack took a moment to think. What was he doing? As much as he wanted to help this man, he couldn't. He had his own family to think of.

"I'm sorry, but I can't help you," Jack told him, turned, and strode away.

"Please," Eric pleaded, plodding after Jack, struggling to keep pace with him.

"I have my own shit to take care of."

"But they have my girlfriend if you can help–"

Jack stopped, turning forcefully and suddenly toward Eric.

"I'm sorry to break this to you, Eric. But if they have your girlfriend, she is dead. I haven't seen them take any prisoners. They aren't capturing people, they are killing them."

"No... you're wrong... I saw them drag her away. If they wanted to kill her, why did they drag her away?"

"I'm sorry."

Jack turned and walked away again. Eric ran after him and pulled him back once more, causing Jack to turn around and talk through gritted teeth.

"I cannot help you."

"Please," Eric offered, eyes full of fear. "I'm trapped here. I'm all alone. I just need some help."

Jack sighed. He looked around, considering his time limits, considering his family, considering the passage into the city – so much at stake.

"This is my offer, take it or leave it," Jack confidently asserted. "I have a way you can get out of the city. Come with me, and you can do that. But that is it. You do not slow me down for a moment."

"But... what about my girlfriend?"

"Your girlfriend is dead, Eric. Now, what's it going to be?"

Jack peered at Eric impatiently, his fists clenching tighter and tighter with each irritating moment.

"Okay," Eric eventually nodded, drying further tears from his face.

Jack turned and charged forward, annoyed he had wasted twenty seconds he could have used to get back to his family. He wasn't far now. Just around the corner.

He continued onward with tunnel vision, vacantly listening to Eric's messy steps trying to keep up.

CHAPTER THIRTY-NINE

SUNIYA'S back spasmed with immense pain as she slammed into the side of the van. As the vehicle swung around another corner, she did all she could to grip the floor and keep herself steady but failed once more.

The man with the scar stood over her, watching with a knowing grin. He held onto the side of the van to keep himself steady, watching Suniya struggle with a menacing chuckle.

"How long?" the man barked, banging on the window between them and the driver's seat.

"Five minutes!" was the reply.

"Five minutes?" The man beamed at Suniya. "Do you know what we can do in five minutes?"

Suniya used the side of the van to drag herself to her feet, throwing herself against the back doors. She grabbed hold of the door with both hands and tried to open it. She pulled, she pushed, she twisted, she did everything she could possibly think of, but it was no good.

She was alone with this man.

"Sit down," he told her.

"No," Suniya snarled defiantly, pressing herself up against the wall, as far away from him as she could.

He withdrew a large, rounded blade and held it out to her.

"Sit the fuck down," he repeated.

She used the walls to lower herself to the ground.

"On your knees with your hands behind your back," he enforced.

She did as she was told.

He grinned.

"Open your mouth."

Suniya narrowed her eyes.

"Open it," he repeated, brandishing the blade once more.

She complied, her eyes glaring at him as she did.

He burst out laughing. "Hah! Oh, my fuckin' God. You lot are all so uptight, covering your hair 'cause men can't see 'em, covering your body from head to toe, ankles being covered up and all that shit. But it's all a front. When it comes down to it, you are on your knees with a mouth open ready for a cock, you're still the filthy bitches every fuckin' ho in this country is."

Continuing his laugh, he picked some rope off the ground and made his way behind Suniya.

Suniya watched, never taking her eyes off him. Wary of every movement. Cautious of what he did with his hands.

Whatever he thought he was going to do to her, he was not. He would have another thing coming. She would fight, and she would bite, and she would do whatever she had to in order to keep her dignity.

"Keep your fuckin' mouth open," he told her, holding his head next to her ear as he bound her hands tightly behind her with the rope.

Holding her mouth open with rigid muscles, she did as she was told.

Once he had finished tying her hands, he stood in front of her. Looking down at her. Condescending to her humiliated state. A disgusting, perverted, cocky laugh escaping from his cracked lips.

She struggled to get her hands loose, to see if there was any leeway. She could barely move them. They were done tightly, the rope interweaved around her wrists, ensuring a complete lack of maneuverability.

"You ain't getting out of those fuckers," he laughed, a dirty, wicked grin making her shudder. "This ain't the first time I've tied a bird's hands behind her back."

"So what?" Suniya spat. "You did this whole thing just to rape me? Why don't you just kill me and get it over with?"

"Oh no, no, no. I ain't gon' kill you. That's for Bruno. You're gon' be the martyr."

With his fat, filthy hand, he grabbed hold of her hijab and pulled. Feeling its tight security, he pulled it back and forth, waving her head with it.

She pulled her head back and took her hijab out of his grasp, glaring up at him. Her eyes were full of venom, ready to fight whatever he wanted to do.

"Get off me!"

He withdrew his blade once more and held it beside her throat, speaking slowly and precisely.

"If you move your mouth from being wide open once more, I will cut it."

A solitary tear escaped her eye.

Fighting was no good.

Not with a blade that size.

To survive, she had to endure.

He grabbed hold of her hijab with one hand and, with the other, stuck the blade through. With a few back and forth movements, he had peeled the hijab off her head and ripped it in two.

He flung it to the ground beside her.

A smug smile made her fill with dread as he looked down at her long, beautiful, wavy hair.

Her hair was not for him.

It was for Eric.

Eric, who had deserted her. Eric, who did nothing to stop this.

"You know…" He stuck out his bottom lip and gave a repulsive nod of his head in confirmation of his repulsive thoughts. "You are actually a pretty fit bird when you get rid of all this Muslim shit. If it weren't for this headscarf, this whole covering every bit of you up, ah'd a fucked you. Ah'd a fucked you so good."

Taking her hair in his hand, he lifted her head up, forcing an anxious whimper to escape her delicate lips.

Sliding the blade under the bottom of her dress, she felt its sharp point rest against her thigh. He dragged the blade slowly up, bringing her dress up with it, inch by humiliating inch.

She closed her eyes.

Scrunched up her face.

Pressed her eyelids firmly against each other.

What she'd give to be anywhere else but there. What if she'd stayed in Birmingham that morning? With her family?

What if Eric had helped her?

What if a lot of things had happened?

Just as her dress reached the line of her underwear, she felt the van grind to a sudden halt.

He planted his lips against her ear, causing an uncomfortable shiver to tremble through her, shuddering her shoulders. She was very aware of the blade beside her crotch and the closeness of this man's heavy, heaving body against hers.

"We're here," he whispered.

He threw her to the floor.

Despite being bound behind her, she still managed to clamber her hands desperately over her dress, pulling it down, covering herself up, preserving whatever dignity she could still cling to.

He grinned. That same masochistic, shuddering grin, illuminating his scar.

"Don't get too comfortable," he instructed her. "The best is yet to come."

With that, the doors to the van flung open and she was dragged out. No matter how much she fought and threw her limbs about, there were too many of them.

She was overpowered.

CHAPTER FORTY

ERIC'S FEET trudged heavily through the stained puddles. His trainers were a muddy mess but he didn't care.

All he could see was Suniya.

Her face as she was dragged away.

That final look.

How could he live with himself? He had let the woman he loves get carried away by two sadistic murderers – and did nothing.

Then again, if he did something, maybe he'd be dead too.

Fuck it, I die too, so be it.

At least he'd be able to face himself.

He imagined Suniya's final moments. The terrified look in her eyes as the scarred man's blade carved into her skin.

Her final thoughts. Dwelling on the boyfriend she wished she'd never known. The coward who let her go.

That was the only word he could use to describe himself.

Coward.

There was still a niggling thought, an incessant bugging possibility, etched in the back of his mind.

If they were going to kill her, why not do it there and then? Everyone else was killed on the spot – why drag her away?

What were they planning to do to her?

He ended that train of thought immediately, not able to bear the possibilities.

Distracting himself from his overactive mind, he focussed on the man he was following, fervently charging ahead whilst Eric traipsed behind.

Who was he?

Where had he come from?

And he was black. How had he survived?

"So, who are you, anyway?" Eric mused, rushing to the man's side.

"My name's Jack. Jack Taylor." The man didn't break stride or shift his tunnel vision whatsoever. "I'm a police constable. At least, I was, an hour ago."

"So why aren't the police doing anything about this? Where is the police force?"

Jack turned to Eric with a longing grin. "You're looking at it."

"I don't understand."

"They are dead, Eric. Every police station was taken out right at the beginning of this – I don't know, whatever this is – and all my friends were murdered."

"So how come you escaped?"

"You're asking too many questions."

Before Eric could persist any further, Jack quickly shoved a hand across his new comrade's chest and shoved him up against the wall. He took a position beside Eric.

Jack peered around the corner, squinting into the distance.

In an abrupt moment, his body tensed, stiffening with dread. His eyes widened and his mouth turned into a horrifying snarl.

"You fucker," he growled.

Without any warning, he sprinted out from his hiding position as quickly as his speedy legs would take him.

Eric peered around the corner and watched in terror.

Jack withdrew a meat cleaver from the back of his belt and raised it into the air. He approached at pace, skidding to a halt, screaming nonsensical, aggressive remarks.

A man clothed with a balaclava held a small child in his arms. He sadistically laughed as he repeatedly tossed the toddler up in the air, chuckling as he grabbed hold of the little girl's ankle, stopping her from narrowly missing the ground at the last moment. Next to him, his mate laughed cockily, finding it uproariously funny that this man was tormenting a small, black child.

Before them was a woman, on her knees, evidently the child's distressed, dismayed mother.

Jack took no time in launching himself forward, lifting his weapon into the air, and landing it straight through the collar of the man toying with the child.

With his spare hand, Jack ripped the child away from the assailant and handed her to the weeping mother, who clutched her child in her arms.

Jack withdrew his weapon and, before the wounded man could retaliate, plunged it upwards through the side of the tormentor's rib and into his heart.

Sliding the blade out, he stuck it into the other man's neck and slid it out, forcing that man to fall heavily to the ground.

Jack dropped his weapon, splattered with thick blood, and embraced the woman and child. Holding them tightly, squeezing them, grasping for dear life, he allowed tears to flow.

Eric imagined they were tears of relief.

Jack's family was safe. His child, the woman he loved, was safe.

Because he jumped out and launched himself at those attacking the woman he loves. He did whatever it took. He was brave.

Eric wished he was Jack.

CHAPTER FORTY-ONE

Pride devoured Bruno's thoughts, like a spider devouring its prey.

Everything he had managed, everything he had accomplished. All the organisations, the references, the experience of the people. The sheer ambition of the project. The complete neglect of his family for the year it had taken him to put this day together. The absolute indescribable feeling of joy to see it all come off.

This was what he'd dreamt of when he joined the English Hearts.

So many people quit because of him. Said he was too extreme. Said he was racist.

He's not racist.

Don't be a fucking punk.

He is a patriot. A nationalist. A loyal member of the United Kingdom.

And they were being attacked.

With weapons? No.

With tools far more lethal than weapons.

In the country's law. In the jobs, the welfare state, in the place of English people who would otherwise have business.

In the infrastructure.

Stoke-on-Trent had an Indian member of parliament. A fucking immigrant as a politician. A fucking immigrant infiltrating the powers and rulers of the country.

It was not their country to infiltrate.

It was Bruno's country.

My fucking country.

And now, he had taken it back. Taken it all right back. Sucked the country back from the leeches who bombarded it from abroad.

From the Muslims.

The fucking Muslims.

The Muslims who killed innocent people.

9/11.

7/7.

Fucking ISIS on the fucking beach of fucking France.

Celebrating when his people die.

Cunts, the lot of them. A bunch of smarmy, murderous, filthy cunts.

And now, they returned this city to its rightful inhabitants. It would never make it up, never even out the numbers. But it was a start.

The most multicultural city in England.

Multicultural. Pah!

Multicultural is just a term given to a place with too many immigrants in it.

Last time India beat Britain in the cricket, the Indians ransacked the streets. Danced on the roads with their flags, making *British* people late for their *British* jobs working for *fucking immigrants.*

Who's laughing now?

The bloodshed had been magnificently ruthless.

And now, standing on the top floor of the Potteries,

surveying his busy minions organising and supporting, he stood strong. Looked down upon the various dedicated English Hearts members scurrying about their jobs.

"Boss," came the familiar, gruff voice of one of his highest generals beside him.

Bruno turned to his side and feasted his eyes upon the blood-stained clothes of Pearson. The man's scar, prominently pronounced down his face, always made him excited at the brilliance of this man's savagery.

Pearson was a sadistic fucker, and Bruno used him as such. Pearson was the only member of the English Hearts Bruno could rely on to always get the vile, detestable murder done.

"How's it goin'?" Bruno smirked.

As he said it, he spotted a bracelet in the shop behind Pearson. He hurried over to it, clambered over the smashed window, and picked it up. He placed it in his pocket and turned back to Pearson.

"For ma daughter, she loves this shit," Bruno announced. "What have you got for me?"

"Oh, boss, great exalted leader," Pearson playfully cackled, "how you are goin' to love me."

"What is it?"

"You know your martyr? That bird with the fancy headscarf and the fancy bitchy body?"

"Yes?" Bruno stepped up excitedly, shaking like a boy at Christmas.

"We got her," Pearson confirmed. "*I* got her."

Bruno flew his arms around Pearson and squeezed him into a tight embrace, patting his back, demonstrating his sheer elation.

"You son of a bitch!" Bruno smirked, punching Pearson on the arm as a triumphant declaration of admiration.

"You know it, boss."

"Where is she?"

"Bringin' her up now."

Bruno directed his eyes to the ground floor.

There, he saw a Muslim girl, tears streaming down her filthy, brown cheeks, a lining of her hijab around her head, with torn pieces of cloth outlining a wave of luscious, black hair. Her elegant dress was ripped up her leg, a sure sign that Pearson had tampered with her.

She looked distraught. Inconsolable.

Pathetic.

Idiotic.

A terrorist.

A dirty fucker.

"She's perfect," Bruno declared.

CHAPTER FORTY-TWO

THE HARSHNESS of the hot water brought Eric's senses back to life. Shovelling cupped hands of water from the sink to his face, he used it to stimulate his mind back. To restore him from his neglectful catatonic state.

Lifting his head, he looked himself in the mirror.

It was the same face he was used to.

The same acne scars. The same greasy hair. The same geeky glasses over his dopey eyes.

The same chin hair that only grew into fluff despite being a nineteen-year-old man.

The same sweaty brow that gave away any feeling of anxiety he felt – which was practically *all the time*.

The same blue eyes. The same eyes Suniya had gazed into. The same eyes she had been looking at the first time she told him that she loved him.

Those eyes broke.

His demeanour fell, his lip quivered and, before he knew it, he was blubbering like a child.

He ran his hands through his hair, his vision compromised by the blurred water flooding from his tear ducts.

He bent over and screamed.

It felt good, screaming. Letting it out.

Letting his emotions verbalise themselves into an angry roar.

He'd never heard himself sound angry before. He was always so terrified of sounding angry, in case it offended someone and made someone angry with him. Anger leads to conflict.

Eric had always hated conflict.

Conflict got you hurt. Got your nose broken. Got your arm bruised. Got your lungs winded.

I am pathetic.

He screamed again, angry at the thought, dismayed at the inescapable truth that he was a cowardly child too scared of bloody everything to ever live a proper, content, bloody life.

Stop being so pathetic, then. Stop it. Stop it, you incessant, irritable prick.

But he couldn't.

He'd let her go. He'd watched her as she was dragged away. Kicking and screaming. Her eyes beseeching him to help.

Those eyes.

Those damn, bloody eyes.

He kicked the door open and strode into the hallway, looking back and forth at this family home.

The child's room, so perfectly decorated, with toys organised neatly on shelves – something he would no longer get to have with Suniya.

The grand bedroom with a tidy double bed, where a happy couple would lie together – that he would no longer get to have with Suniya.

The spare room for visitors from friends – that he would no longer...

Friends. Eric wished he had the guts to have friends.

Treading heavily downstairs, he made his way into the living room.

His steps ceased. He stopped abruptly, looking at the beautiful sight before him.

Jack sat on the floor, his child on his lap, his wife to his side. Looking at each other with eyes full of complete adoration. The child was flicking through a book. The wife was stroking her hand down Jack's hair. Jack was smiling.

Sincerely, definitely, unequivocally smiling.

Alerted to Eric's presence, Jack turned toward him.

"Hey, Eric, you ready to go?"

Eric looked upon this family.

The dream. A happy, close-knit unit of support. Together, they faced anything.

No need to be afraid of conflict.

No need to be a coward.

"I'm not going with you," Eric announced, strong in his decision.

"What?" Jack replied, confused.

"I'm going back. I'm going back for Suniya."

Jack looked to his family and nodded, promising he'd be back in a few moments, and dragged Eric into the other room.

"What are you on about?" Jack asked.

"I've got to go back for her," Eric asserted, assured in his convictions. "I've been a coward. I have to."

"Eric, man, I don't want to have to say this – but she is probably dead. You know that, right?"

"Sure." Eric looked away for a moment, stifling tears. "But I don't think she is. I have to go after her."

"Eric –"

"What would you do? If it was your wife, what would you do?"

Jack held Eric's eyes for a moment, contemplating him, considering the strong, confident look forced upon the young man's face.

In a quick turn, he opened a drawer and withdrew something. Eric's jaw dropped.

"Take this," Jack told Eric, shoving a pistol into his hands.

"Don't you need it?"

"I've got weapons, I'm fine. I wasn't going to take it anyway."

Eric mulled the gun over. Dread came over him.

"I don't even know where to go. What to do."

"This is what I'd suggest," Jack started, putting his hand on Eric's shoulder. "The Potteries, the shopping centre. It's the hive of everything for them. It's where they are running things. Go there. If they took her somewhere, it would be there."

"How do I get in?"

"You have a distinct advantage, Eric – you are white. You can pass as one of them. Use that. Just…"

"What?"

Jack sighed in hesitation.

"Be confident with it. Or it won't work. Be a scumbag, be one of them – or they won't believe it."

Eric looked thoughtfully at the weapon in his hands, then tucked it into the back of his waist. He had never held a gun before. With everything that was happening, it was just another action that overwhelmed his fragile mind.

"I don't know what to say," Eric announced. "Thank you."

Jack smiled, pulled Eric in close, and they embraced in a momentary, manly hug.

Then Jack pulled away, grabbed his bag, ensured his meat cleavers were tucked into the back of his waist, and hustled his family out the door.

Eric was alone.

Completely, utterly alone.

Time to be brave.

CHAPTER FORTY-THREE

THE KICKS WOUNDED HER RIBS.

The punches blackened her eyes.

The scratches made her bleed from the most painful parts of her body.

But what hurt Suniya the most was the complete, debilitating humiliation she suffered at the hands of these racist miscreants.

What point were they trying to make by beating a helpless, distressed young woman?

What, because her skin wasn't the same as theirs? Nor her religion?

These thoughts quickly escaped her mind and defence mechanisms jumped into place. She wrapped her arms around her head and her neck, curling her body into a ball.

It still hurt.

Sure, she covered her chest. The boots still laid into her back. Again and again and again and again and again.

The one second she could lift her head, searching for somewhere to run, an escape she could go to, she regretted it. The heel of a large boot landed into her nose and a long moan escaped her bleeding lips.

She became used to it. The punching, the kicking. The crowd around her adamant in beating her until there was nothing left.

They had already stripped her of her hijab.

Her belly felt a sudden painful queasiness at the thought. These people were successfully degrading her, taking away everything she was. As she felt a hand creep over her thigh in the melee of arms flailing around her, she projectile vomited a mouthful of bloody lumps.

The crowd around her stopped. An abrupt pause in their bombardment.

Slowly, she lifted herself to her knees, spitting a mouthful of blood that lingered on her lip and hovered in a trail of gunk to the floor.

As she crouched, allowing her wounded chest to resume coherent breaths, the aches became quickly apparent. Her body's numbing of the pain, protecting herself against the assaults, ended with the attacks. Despite the melee around her no longer throwing punches and kicks, the pain consumed her. Everything agonised.

Her arms she used to steady herself gave way; her muscles deadened, her elbows weak. She allowed her head to drop to the floor, keeping her knees in position. She realised this meant her posterior was risen into the air and, fearing attack from more perverted members of the organisation, she fell onto her thigh and lay on her side.

Sobbing.

Longing for help.

Longing for release.

The crowd before her parted. Her body convulsed in terrified shakes as the man with the scar strolled forward, a folded gown in his hand.

He knelt before her. Before he could speak, Suniya was already backing away.

"Don't you touch me," she scolded. The beating was one thing, but if anyone thought they were going to touch her, they would have a rabid fight on their hands.

"Please," the scarred man replied. "We are not that kind of organisation. No one is going to rape you."

"What you did in the van said otherwise." Suniya scowled.

"My name is Pearson," the man smiled, revealing a scatter of grills inside his salivating mouth. "I am part of the English Hearts. We don't sexually abuse people."

"No, just drag them out onto the streets and kill them."

"If you are the ones taking over our country, then yes."

"*Taking over your country?*"

Pearson chuckled knowingly, shaking his head as a mocking gesture. He threw the gown at her feet.

"Put this on."

Suniya picked it up. It was a large, white gown. On the centre of the front and back were the words *English Hearts*, along with the organisation's logo.

"You want me to wear this?"

"I'm not asking."

Suniya sighed. If this was what kept her alive. If this was what kept her unmolested.

"Fine," she resolved. "Where shall I get changed?"

Pearson stood up and held his hands out, looking up and down the shopping centre, indicating this was as good a place as any.

"I'm not getting undressed here," Suniya growled through gritted teeth.

A gun instantly pressed into the back of her head, sending a shiver of fear down Suniya's body like a volt of electricity.

"You won't kill me," Suniya gasped. "You need me for something."

"Please. There are plenty of birds out there I can get if you ain't willing."

Suniya looked Pearson deep into his eyes.

He meant it.

She precariously rose to her feet, struggling to keep balance, her deadened legs seizing and throbbing with pain.

Grasping the gown, she looked around. All the men that were gathered into a circle, beating her, looked back. A few dozen. With guns, knives, blades. Some of their faces masked, some of their vile visages visible, gaping at her with depraved grins.

She dropped her head. Closed her eyes. Wished she was somewhere else.

This was because she was a Muslim.

To them, Muslim women are closed off, out of bounds. They don't drink. They dress modestly. They cover up their hair, as it is something precious to the man they love.

This was their opportunity.

To see a young, pretty, Muslim woman stripped and degraded.

It was warped entertainment for them.

And she had never felt this low in her entire life.

"Clock's tickin'..." sang Pearson.

Keeping her head bowed, focussing on a circle of dried gum ingrained into the floor, she found herself obeying.

She slipped one hand beneath her dress strap and slid it down her arm. Then she slipped one hand beneath the other dress strap and slid that one down too.

She closed her eyes and took in a deep breath. She sniffed, stifling a tear. She would not give them that.

They did not deserve her tears.

She focussed on the squashed gum. Focussed on the ground beneath her so she didn't see any of their sick eyes leering at her.

She dropped her dress to her feet and stepped out of it.

She could feel them. Even though she wouldn't look at them, they were there, in the corner of her eye. She couldn't see Pearson's grin, but she could feel it, she could hear its debauched enjoyment.

Her underwear matched. It was black and lacy. Because it was for Eric. For that night.

She had bought this underwear especially for him, and this was the first night she was wearing it.

Eric.

Where are you? How could you let me go?

She lifted the gown over her head and dropped it to the floor, encompassing her body in the twisted robes of the English Hearts.

Carefully, her face rose, her eyes peering on Pearson ahead of her.

He was sitting there, leant against a water fountain, his eyes leering at her intently.

"See, now that weren't so bad, was it?" he jested.

"What are you going to do to me now?"

Pearson stepped forward and placed a condescending arm around her shoulder, pointing behind her. She turned and looked at a large wooden spike with a rope attached to it, and wooden logs at the base.

"That," Pearson declared.

"What? What is it?"

"That," Pearson continued, "is an item of beauty. And you are going to be the finishing bow."

"She's perfect!" rang out a joyful voice that sounded too familiar to Suniya.

Suniya spun around.

It was him.

The man who had killed Ahmad.

Walking toward her with his arms open wide as if she was a distant relative he was becoming acquainted with once again.

Bruno Tug.

CHAPTER FORTY-FOUR

An extra-wary sense of vigilance had descended on Jack's mind. Before, he was caring for himself. Though he cared about whether he got back to his family, he wasn't too fussed about the risk he was taking.

Now, he flinched at every rustle of leaves. Jolted at every lingering haze of smoke travelling through the air. Alert at any flicker of light.

Vanessa had Tallah strapped to her chest with a sling. Even though she looked uncomfortably big for it now, and it was an uncomfortable weight on Vanessa, it was the best way to transport her. She was asleep, and soundly so. If she wasn't making any noise or asking any of her wondrous questions, they had a better chance of not being noticed.

Jack would have carried her, relishing the closeness – but he needed the bag of weapons he had thrown over his back. This bag was heavy and was his burden to carry.

Jack concealed himself and his family under the shadow of a tall building and dropped his bag on the floor. Once his wife had safely nestled herself on the floor against the wall, his child safely asleep, he opened his bag and rummaged through.

He withdrew a Glock 45 and checked the ammunition. A full load. Ready for any surprises. He tucked it securely into his waistband.

This was followed by a screwdriver, which he tucked into his back pocket.

Reaching into the bag once more, he withdrew his radio and, glancing back and forth down the dim street, barely lit by the generosity of the moon, he turned the volume dial up ever so slightly and put it to his mouth.

"This is PC Taylor, come in, over," he spoke, in a thoroughly professional manner.

A few moments passed where he received nothing but static, then finally a voice came through.

"Good to hear you, PC Taylor, this is First Lieutenant Anders. Are you ready to receive, over?"

Jack glanced over his shoulder.

There they were. His loving family. The sleeping head of his beautiful child, the scared but loving eyes of his devoted wife.

He was filled with adoration. For so much of his life, he had thought he was defined by what he achieved as a police officer. He was wrong.

This was how he was defined.

By a wondrous, beautiful family.

Vanessa looked at him with the same loving look, mixed with anxiety and worry.

She was ready to leave.

She didn't know he was not going with them.

"Confirmed, are you ready to receive mine, over?"

"Roger, over."

Jack checked the coast was clear once more, gave a patient nod to Vanessa, and crept forward into the middle of the street.

Never had he felt more exposed.

Flat blocks and offices ran down either side of the street, sailing high into the air of the city. Any window could house a man with a gun. That would be all it took, and it was operation over, his family gone.

He scanned every window. So many shadows, so much darkness, he couldn't be sure. It was a risk.

Every single part of this plan was a risk.

Crouching down and placing the radio on the floor, he reached into his back pocket and withdrew the screwdriver. Firmly pressing it into the screws around the drain beside the curb, he undid the first screw, the second, the third.

He scanned the street once more. Looked past every blackened window that surrounded him.

Listened carefully.

He undid the fourth, the fifth, then the sixth.

Placing the screwdriver to the side, he reached his fingers down and hooked the drain up, placing it to his side.

He reached a hand down and clasped it around the hand of Lieutenant Anders. Anders was a muscular man with a stylish goatee and a confident demeanour. Just the man you would want leading you to your potential death.

Once the four soldiers that followed were out, Anders directed them to a side street, where they scarpered to and took cover.

Looking down, Jack saw another man reaching his hands up from the messy abyss below.

Giving a wave to his family, Vanessa took Tallah and rushed over to him.

"Are you ready?" Jack asked.

Vanessa nodded nervously.

Jack took Tallah from her. She began to stir, and Jack planted a delicate kiss on her forehead.

"Hey, baby," he smiled at her.

"Daddy?"

"You're going to go somewhere with Mummy now, okay?"

She looked confused. Terrified. Jack needed to pass her on,

or he would never let her go. He reluctantly passed her to the army general below, withdrawing his arm from her outstretched hand, trying not to falter at the mortified expression on her face. She looked betrayed.

Once she had been taken down, the man reached up once more.

"Vanessa," Jack turned to his wife, taking her hand.

"Jack?" she answered, loyally.

"Go with these men. They will take you and Tallah to safety."

"You mean, you're not coming with us?"

Jack could feel his eyes welling up.

This was his family.

But this was also his job. His responsibility.

His duty.

"I know where they are," he desperately justified, clasping her hand in his, stroking his hand passionately down the side of her face. "I know what their targets look like, they need me. Without me, this operation won't be so successful."

"But, Jack… what about me? Tallah?"

"I'm coming back."

"What if you don't?"

He looked into her weak, despairing eyes.

"PC Taylor, we need to go," urged Anders from behind Jack.

Jack gave her no verbal answer.

Instead, he wrapped his arms around her as tightly as he could. He felt his hand sprawl out and grab onto the back of her top, squeezing tightly, holding her, taking in her scent in case he never smelt it again. He felt her arms around him, feeling the warmth, the security, the special feeling he got when her arms were around him that he was indestructible.

Twenty years, and he had never lost that feeling.

"I love you," he told her.

"I love you, too," she sobbed through fatal tears.

And that was it.

Jack ripped himself away, the man took her into the gutter, and the drain was screwed back into place.

Jack joined Anders and the four stealthy men who had ventured into this operation.

And he prayed it would not be the last time he ever told her he loved her.

CHAPTER FORTY-FIVE

Eric had never had swagger.

Eric was a geeky, white, middle-class man with no street credentials whatsoever. He had never used a colloquialism in his life that had come from a place of slang or informal language.

Eric was not a lad. He was a man in-as-much as he was born that way, but his interests had been theatre. Musicals. Superheroes. Comics. Books. Lord of the Rings. Harry Potter. Batman.

Eric had a fleeting interest in football, but would never have had the guts to join in a derogatory chant at a match, nor shout abuse at a referee.

He was a timid, intelligent, but anxious young man.

All his life he had been terrified of pissing someone off. Terrified of winding someone up the wrong way, saying the wrong thing, giving someone the wrong look – anything that would mean they hurt him. He was terrified of getting punched, breaking a bone, or even getting his hands slightly dirty.

But that had to stop.

It all had to stop immediately.

He was going to become that person he was so terrified of.

He was going to have to take that swagger, that language, that intimidating glare. He was going to have to lose that fear of getting hurt.

His middle-class voice and nervous walk into every situation – it was going to have to go.

Enough was enough.

He acquired a black tracksuit from a store that had been smashed to pieces and savagely looted. Tucking sports socks over the bottom of the tracksuit bottoms, he then lifted his hood up.

He had never looked badass with his hood up. At best, he had looked dry. Sheltered from the rain.

Attempting a slight limp, a slight swank in his walk, he approached the Potteries.

Then froze.

There were masses of them, stretched as far as he could see. Dressed like him. With weapons. Aggression. Anger.

What was he doing?

I can't be one of them.

He couldn't pull this off.

It was no good.

He knew it. He would die. They would all have a good laugh, a hearty guffaw at the hilarity of his predicament, and send him straight to death.

Then he heard a scream.

A woman's scream. Piercing, clear as day, soaring through the heavy night.

He would know that voice anywhere.

It was Suniya's scream.

Fuck it. Man up. Too late to back out now.

Attempting an embarrassing slant to his walk once more, he sauntered up to the entrance and peered in. He opened the door and immediately two men shoved Stanley knives to his throat.

"What are you doin'?" one of them demanded.

"Mate, I'm here for the thing, yeah?" Eric had never called someone mate in his life.

"Where you meant to be stationed?" the man prompted, glancing at Eric's waist.

Why was he glancing at Eric's waist?

Oh shit, they all have radios.

"Lost my radio, didn't I?" Eric answered, attempting to pass for one of them by using the worst grammar he could.

"So why you 'ere?" The man scrunched his nose into a malicious snarl, growling his question in Eric's face.

The man's grip on the Stanley knife grew tighter.

Eric had the gun tucked into the back of his belt.

But he couldn't use it. If the people inside heard a gunshot, they'd come running and he'd be dead in seconds.

Still, the Stanley knife sent fear jolting up and down his spine. His arms shook vigorously and he willed them to stop. It was a character. He had to believe it.

He had to be confident.

He had to sell the idea to this guy that he was meant to be there.

"I..." he began, trailing off, quivering once more.

Got to be confident.

"I lost my fuckin' radio, you cunt!" Eric barked, startling himself by his uproarious use of vile language. "Nah get that fuckin' knife out my face, would you? I'm here for..."

He trailed off.

What was he there for?

The guy looked at him expectantly.

Was he buying it?

Shit, what am I here for?

Then he remembered.

What the scarred man had said. As they left, what he had called Suniya.

"I'm here for the martyr, ain't I?" Eric declared.

The man lowered his Stanley knife and moved aside, allowing Eric in.

He'd done it.

Then he saw the vast army before him.

I haven't done anything yet.

So many people. So many weapons.

The scarred man. He strode toward Eric. Making a beeline.

"It's Pearson," Eric luckily heard one of the other blokes say.

"Hey, Pearson," Eric greeted, mentally punching himself for the bounciness of his statement.

"Fuck are you 'ere for?"

"Mate, I'm here for the martyr."

Pearson's grin spread across his face.

"Want a front row seat, do ya?" Pearson prompted. "And why the fuck should I give you one, when all these people 'ere didn't even get a ticket?"

"Because..." Eric stuttered.

Shit.

Why should he be able to?

Suniya. He was going to have to speak about Suniya.

"'Cause I tried to get that Muslim bird you got, but she slipped me." Eric half-rose his lip, forcing a cocky slant to his face. "I want to see that bitch burn."

"Gave you the slip, did she?" Pearson laughed. "Fair play, mate, dibs for trying an' all that. Right this way."

Pearson put his arm around Eric's shoulders and led him forward, shooting an angry look at a few men complaining that they didn't get a chance.

"Tell me about this slip she gave you, then," Pearson prompted, keeping his arm draped heavily around Eric's shoulder like they were bosom buddies.

"Well, I thought I had 'er, then she was with this bloke who tackled me an' that. An', er..."

Eric's thoughts weren't moving quickly enough.

Come on, Eric. Come on!

"An', er... so, I killed him. Knifed him in the gut, like. Then she got away, went into some flat block."

"Do you know what, my friend?" Pearson stuck his bottom lip out and nodded his head. "That sounds like bullshit."

Pearson stopped. He turned to Eric, his fists clenched, his head leaning forward, like a lion about to pounce.

"Why don't you tell me who you really are?"

Eric froze.

How could he know?

Pearson hadn't seen him.

Eric's eyes wandered to Pearson's scar, distracted by the war wound. Mortified by it.

His spare hand crept around his back, feeling for the gun.

Ready.

Just in case.

"I'm... Eric," Eric replied.

Fuck. Why use my real name?

He tried not to let his self-anger show on his otherwise pretendedly resolute face.

Pearson peered at him, narrow-eyed, curious.

Then he grinned. Laughed.

"I'm fuckin' with you, Eric. I got respect for someone who tried to get this bird. She's a fighter, I get you. But don't you worry, my friend, we are going to watch her burn."

Pearson led Eric around the corner, to an openly secluded end of the shopping centre.

A few dozen lucky men gathered.

Bruno Tug, the man Eric had seen kill Ahmad in the alleyway, stood tall. Triumphant. A cocky, knowing grin on his face as he stared at the monument before him.

Eric tried not to let his terror at the sight of this man and the memory of what he had done show.

Then he was rotated around, to look upon the martyr.

Look upon the woman they were going to watch burn, as Pearson said it.

To look upon the eyes of the woman he loves, so close to death.

There she was.

Suniya.

CHAPTER FORTY-SIX

This was more than Suniya could endure.

She wished she'd been killed straight away. She wished she'd been granted the luxury of a quick, meaningless death. As it was, they were going to burn her alive and make an example out of her.

Because she was young.

Because she was a woman.

And a Muslim.

Her fight had left her. She was reluctant to kick out, to punch back. What was the point? She was surrounded by numerous armed psychopaths. All it would do is spur them on more. They seemed to be getting turned on by her resilience.

So she held her hands behind her back.

Bent over on her knees, letting them do whatever.

A pair of handcuffs fastened around her wrists, digging into the bones at the base of her hand, giving her a permanent discomfort she was going to have to become acclimatised to.

Once they were done, she didn't move.

She didn't even cry anymore.

Why bother?

Crying wouldn't make them stop. Wouldn't make death any less inevitable. Wouldn't make the humiliating torture she was about to endure any less drastic or extreme.

She just wished her last sight of someone who loved her wasn't that of Eric watching her get dragged away.

Dragged away to this.

A sweaty hand gripped her hair and dragged her forward. She tried moving her legs to keep up with the pace of this man, something to stop it hurting. But she couldn't.

So she just let herself be dragged. Feeling clumps of hair fall out in this man's fist.

Thrown onto the floor, she looked up at the soon-to-be effigy before her.

A wooden stake.

Like a witch. Like a witch, from five hundred years ago.

This was how backward they were.

They were using medieval torture methods on her, in response to her believing something different to them.

History always repeats itself.

And, unfortunately, history is always written by those who win.

The English Hearts were winning. They would write this history. And they will celebrate this day, make it a bank holiday, a landmark in their history.

And she would be the centre of their celebration.

With no help from her unbalancing hands held firmly behind her back, she meandered her way to her knees and looked up at the monument in which she would die.

"Brilliant, innit?" came a rough, familiar voice next to her.

She looked to her side, up at the conceited face of Bruno Tug. His feet confidently shoulder-width apart, a prominent, alpha male stance.

She hated this. On her knees, looking up at him, like some sick, twisted victim of porn.

She felt pathetic.

"You're part of something big," Bruno continued, an uncaged, elated smirk upon his face. "Part of something grand, something massive. You should be proud."

"Fuck you," Suniya muttered.

Why not?

If she was going to die, she may as well not hold back.

Bruno laughed at her reaction, chuckling like a child had just offered a foolish comment because that child just didn't understand the adult's reasoning.

"What's your name?" Bruno enquired.

"Suniya."

"Fuck me, that's a proper Muslim name, that is."

"And so what? So what if it is a Muslim name? We've done nothing wrong."

"Done nothing wrong? Al Qaeda? ISIS? What, those Muslims done nothin' wrong?"

"This may surprise you," Suniya venomously spat. "But not every Muslim is a member of a terrorist organisation. Most of us are good, honest people, doing nothing to hurt you."

"Pah!" Bruno guffawed. "Your kids will go to school with my kids. They'll be exposed to you. And you're telling me you do no harm?"

"And you don't think killing every Muslim you see is worse?"

Bruno crouched and ran a sinister hand down her solemn cheek. She flinched her head away, refusing to let him, glaring at him intently. His disgusting, tortoise-like neck folded on each movement, his wolf-like eyes laughing at her. It was feeding time at the zoo, and he was the ruler of the pack.

"We're cleansing our country of the filth that's been dragged in on the shoes of good people."

Giving her a shove of the head, Bruno turned around and barked, "What are you waiting for? We've got a girl to burn!"

Two men instantly burst forward and manhandled Suniya to

her feet. They dragged her to the giant wooden spike and fastened her to it.

"Wait for me!" sang out a joyful, approaching voice.

Pearson loomed closer, his irritating swagger and menacing scar jaunting toward them. He had someone with him.

Someone Suniya recognised.

Her breath caught in her throat. Her heart raced.

What?

Eric?

Eric approached with a swagger she had never seen from him before, a cocky strut. He had changed. Something was different,

"This the paki bitch?" Eric eagerly enquired.

Oh my God. How could I be so stupid?

Suniya's eyes went. Her resolve fell.

Eric was with them all along.

He was one of them.

She made a brief eye contact with him, then looked away.

"Here she is, my friend," Pearson announced, gesturing toward Suniya.

"Lovely," Eric confirmed. "Can't fucking wait."

Then something happened.

Something very brief, very small – but of overwhelming comfort to Suniya.

Eric winked at her.

A sly, barely noticeable wink.

Then Suniya knew.

He wasn't one of them. He wasn't an English Heart, a racist, a scumbag.

Not to her, anyway.

He had come.

She couldn't believe it.

She had never seen him be so brave.

CHAPTER FORTY-SEVEN

Flickers of rain pattered Jack's face. His cannon held by his side as he crept along the road in swift formation, directly behind Anders.

Glancing over his shoulder, he glanced at the four army personnel joining him on this mission.

The army, like the police force, forced companionship. You had no choice but to be loyal and supportive of the soldiers fighting by your side. But these men already knew each other, already had formed a bond. Working alongside four soldiers that you don't know was difficult at the best of times.

But he was going to have to suck it up.

They were trained marksmen, astute shooters. If they were picked for this mission, they knew what they were doing. And Jack was going to have to trust them.

Anders raised his fist as a gesture for the squad to halt.

"What entrance would you recommend?" Anders asked, turning to Jack.

They had paused on a side street that gave them a concealed view of the main entrance to the Potteries. This was, of course, not an ideal place to enter and attack. Even from the distance they were at, they could see the vast numbers with weapons in there. Despite the English Hearts' potential lack of firearms training compared to the assembled soldiers, hundreds against six were not fathomable odds.

"Our target's Bruno Tug?" Jack asked, musing the possibilities in his mind.

"Roger," Anders confirmed. "We need a better vantage point or a backdoor in."

"Their top floor would likely be sparse. I'd say we scope out the car park, see if that's a better entry, then enter the top floor from there."

"We can't go past the windows, too much of a risk. Is there a way around?"

"Yeah, if we go back down this street and swing around, should be an ETA of three minutes at most, if we're quick."

"Lead the way."

Jack lifted his gun, pointing ahead of him, and edged back down the street. Anders signalled to the rest to follow and they took formation, pursuing him efficiently.

As he led them around the parallel streets, his mind wandered to Vanessa.

The mission was to kill Bruno Tug. But with the numbers in the shopping centre…

They would undoubtedly retaliate.

He understood why so few people had been sent on the mission. Any suspicion, it would fail. A single person who spotted them would ruin everything. An efficient tactical unit that was used to these situations was the best course of action.

But he wasn't part of that unit.

He was a family man. A regular copper.

Pushing through the prominent regret, he willed himself on.

Put those thoughts away, Jack.

Once they had reached the car park, Jack's presumptions had been right – it was sparsely guarded. Two men stood tall outside the pedestrian entrance, and one of the soldiers had taken both these men out with a silencer before Jack had even registered that they were there.

They were through the car park and moving up the stairs within seconds.

Once in, Jack took a position at the back of the line and followed on. The unit was such a well-oiled machine, Jack couldn't help but be impressed. It was clear why they were co-ordinating the operation.

Because they were the best.

Finally reaching the top floor, Anders took a position at the front, edged the door open, peered in, and aimed his gun. Placing a silencer at the end of his weapon in record time, he sent numerous swift bullets floating through the air into what Jack presumed was a gang of men.

Waving everyone in, the rest of the group followed. Jack closed the door behind him and stepped over five or six bodies Anders had managed to easily dispatch.

They took cover in a nearby shop.

They were in.

CHAPTER FORTY-EIGHT

I SHOULD GET an Oscar for this.

A sly wink at Suniya to reassure her whilst sauntering laddishly at Pearson's side.

Is this what it felt like to be a 'lad'?

He was fully in character now. Cocky, arrogant, ready to pretend he hated Suniya.

Only because she knew it was an act.

Only because she knew he was there to save her.

"Sweet little one this, ain't she?" Pearson stood next to Eric with cocksure posture, his back strained and his bottom lip out, admiring his psychopathic work. "Feisty, mind. Gave us a proper good fight. But nothing a few kicks and punches could do, eh?"

"Yeah," Eric agreed, mirroring Pearson's body language, looking down at the Muslim girl in front of him. "Shame I weren't there for it. Wouldn't mind a go."

Pearson sniggered, his snake-like face jiggling in a way that made Eric want to lash out and rip his smirk off.

It was disgusting. But he was doing well. They all thought he was one of them.

His stomach still churned and twisted into painful knots. He had a continuous need to gag, and a frantic voice at the back of his mind gave a constant reminder that he was not one of them.

But he was in character. He was performing well.

Though it did suddenly occur to him.

He had no idea of his next move.

Suniya lay at the base of a large spike, with logs around it, her hands restrained with handcuffs and rope behind her back. Dozens of armed men stood around her in a circle. Pearson was next to him.

And Bruno Tug was next to Suniya. Teasing her. Saying things to her that Eric did not want to hear.

His heart broke in two.

He couldn't stand to watch her there.

Though she was far braver than he, it still hurt. Watching her there, bruised, bleeding, and disgraced.

But he couldn't let that show.

Whatever had been done to her – whatever awful, inescapable atrocities she had endured – he couldn't think about that now. He could think about it later. When she was safe.

When they were both safe.

He could get the image of her humiliated, in pain and looking up with innocent eyes unscarred from his retina later on. But that would come later.

For now, he had to put that feeling aside.

And figure out what he was going to do.

Yes, he had a gun. But so did they.

How was he going to save her?

He could take out his gun and shoot Bruno in the head. A quick shot, a few metres away, straight to the skull.

But then what?

A salvo of bullets would follow, killing both him and any

chance of saving Suniya.

He had gotten this far.

Bruno stood, stretching his back out, turning to Pearson.

"It's time," Bruno declared. "Let's hang her up. Where's Gary and Paul with the matches? We can't set her alight with no matches, can we?"

"They are just coming, boss," Pearson confirmed.

Eric needed to make a decision. Some kind of decision. Something.

They were going to tie her to the spike and burn her. Like a witch in Salem.

The whole 'martyr' thing made sense now.

They were going to sacrifice her.

"Get the camera!" Bruno demanded.

A scuffle broke out from Eric's left, and a group of men brought out a large, industry-standard camera, placing it on a tripod.

They were going to film it.

They are going to film the woman I love burning to death.

And then what?

Use it as propaganda? Use it to make a point to the country? That their hatred has won?

Eric needed to do something.

"Someone lift her up," Bruno demanded. "Someone stand her up for when Gary and Paul get here! I don't want to fuckin' touch her no more."

"Can I have the honour?" Eric piped up.

Can I have the honour? Could I have sounded more middle class?

Bruno turned around and feasted his eyes upon Eric.

"Who the fuck are you?"

"This is my new mate," Pearson interjected. "He's a right lad."

"Fair. A friend ah Pearson's a friend ah mine. Do it."

Eric nodded and stepped forward. He dug his fingers into

Suniya's arms and lifted her up.

"When I start shooting," he whispered to Suniya's ear, so faintly his lips barely moved. "You run."

Shoving her against the spike, his voice turned far louder and aggressive.

"And fuckin' stay there," he instructed her, scrunching his face into a threatening glare.

Just before he took a few steps back and resumed his place alongside Pearson, he dropped his hand to Suniya's.

And gave it a very gentle squeeze.

The same squeeze she would always give him.

The squeeze that would always let him know everything was all right. Suniya's eyes gazed at him with a flicker of hope.

"Right!" Bruno announced. "I think I can see Gary and Paul."

Two men came closer in the distance, carrying a box of lighter fluid, amongst other fatal utensils.

This was it.

He had the element of surprise.

Take out the gun. Fire. By the time bullets had turned on him, Suniya would have had a good head start.

She would make it, at least.

Just as he thought his idea was genius, he froze.

Gary and Paul approached.

Their faces so familiar.

That's when Eric realised.

The pub.

The bathroom.

The two blokes who made fun of his relationship with Suniya.

Approaching.

Staring him straight back in the eye.

And, from their confused expressions, it looked like they recognised Eric, too.

CHAPTER FORTY-NINE

Suniya had no idea what had happened.

One moment, Eric was full of confidence. Portraying the persona of a cocky, arrogant prick perfectly. She was so impressed by him. He had shown bravery she'd never known he had.

But all that bravery had suddenly evaporated. Self-doubt and terror were engraved over his anxious face.

It seemed to be caused by two men approaching, who were being referred to as Gary and Paul.

Two men carrying tanks of creosote and boxes of matches.

Suniya became very aware of Pearson's hand suddenly clamping hard around the back of her neck. A hint of onions stroked her cheek as his croaking, slimy breath pushed against her. She felt it run down her spine, trickling into her blood. It felt dirty. Unclean.

And, aware of the effigy she was mounted to, death had never felt so imminent.

What are you doing, Eric?

Eric's weakened eyes met hers. She could see his tears being willed away, dread consuming his fatal stare.

What was it? What had changed?

Then, as if by a miraculous revelation, the answers gravely unravelled.

"What the fuck are you doin' here?" belligerently barked the one they referred to as Gary, dropping his items to the floor and charging toward Eric.

"Oi!" Pearson shouted. "What's your beef with 'im?"

"Him?" Gary turned to Pearson, posture leant forward, head heavy with aggression, ready for a fight. "He's fuckin' a paki!"

"What?" Bruno interrupted, stepping forward from his place beside Suniya, moving toward Eric.

Eric's hand disappeared behind his back. Suniya could see sweat forming on his brow, a bead of perspiration trickling down his cheek.

He had frozen up. Completely, resolutely, frozen. Stumped.

"This bloke was in a pub earlier, me and Paul were in. He was havin' drinks with his girlfriend, like. His girlfriend was an Islamic."

An Islamic?

"Is this true?" Bruno directed at Eric.

Eric didn't say a word.

Everyone was staring in his direction with wide, anxious eyes. Dozens of men surrounded him, Pearson with his hand gripping Suniya's neck, Gary and Paul rooted to the spot, intensely angry.

Gary's eyes drifted toward Suniya.

His face lit up.

"With her!" he exclaimed.

"What?" Bruno prompted.

"This bloke was in the pub, with 'er. That's 'is bird!"

Bruno shot a dumbfounded glance at Suniya, mouth agape.

Eric was shaking. Suniya could see his knees quivering, his lip trembling, his face twitching.

This was it.

In her final moments, she was going to have to watch him die.

Eric's eyes narrowed.

Intensity met his face with an overwhelming smack.

Something was happening.

A thought was crossing his mind.

It didn't comfort Suniya. It didn't give her faith – if anything, it only unsettled her more.

What is he planning?

"You fuckin' scum," Bruno snarled, his mouth curled, spewing hostility.

Eric closed his eyes for a fleeting moment.

Looking to calm himself.

Then, in one drastic, unprecedented motion, Eric lifted his hand from behind his back, bringing a gun swinging upwards with it.

The gun shaking, shuddering with the tremble of his hand, he directed it at Bruno.

Instantly, the surrounding voyeurs raised every weapon. Masses of guns were pointed at Eric.

Eric's singular gun was pointed at Bruno.

"Anyone so much as brushes their trigger, your leader dies." Eric's voice sounded out, filling the room with a vast echo. Suniya could tell it was an attempt to sound confident and threatening, but it was failing. The shiver in his voice was clearly audible, and Eric did not seem in control.

"Well," Bruno began, forcing a triumphantly masochistic smirk. "Look at this."

"Fuck you," Eric directed at Bruno, trying once again to feign gumption he so sordidly needed.

"Fuck me? We're saving your country from these fuckers, and you're getting your dick wet in one?" Bruno shook his head with an antagonistic tilt.

"You're not saving shit from anyone. All you are is racists. Pure, unadulterated racists."

"Whoa! Those are big words for a little boy who can barely direct his gun."

It was true. Though Eric had taken aim at the man standing only metres away, he wasn't entirely sure he would even be on target, such was the ferocity of his fear.

"Got to say, I'm impressed," Pearson mused with psychopathic hilarity. "For a piece of shit, she is a pretty piece of shit. And you're a fucking weakling."

Pearson took out a large blade and pressed it against Suniya's neck.

"Drop the gun," he demanded. "Or I kill your dirty little girlfriend."

Eric looked into Pearson's eyes.

Feeling the blade against her neck, Suniya could tell Pearson meant it.

But Eric didn't move. Didn't falter. Didn't adjust his position whatsoever.

He kept aiming his gun at Bruno.

CHAPTER FIFTY

A FAINT SQUEAK resounded from Jack's foot as he snuck along the top floor of the shopping centre, concealed in the shadows of burnt-out shops.

One of the soldiers shot him a look.

It was a barely audible sound, the result of his foot brushing the marble floor – but it was far more noise than any of them had made. They were like a silent wind, breezing through, meandering their way efficiently and coolly through the occupied territory.

At the front Anders rose his fist, halting the procession. He used two fingers to gesture that they needed to have eyes below. They all crept forward to gain a better vantage point.

On the bottom floor stood a crowd of English Hearts members. Each of them had a weapon risen, directed at a hazardous scene that stood frozen in the centre of a circle of assailants.

Within that circle stood a large spike behind a young Muslim woman, forced to remain on her knees, her hands bound around the spike behind her back. Next to this woman, a man with a large scar spread across his face held a knife out to the woman's neck.

Then, before the knelt woman, was Bruno Tug.

"Target acquired," confirmed Anders. "Who's that with him?"

Anders looked over his shoulder at Jack, who edged forward for a better vantage point.

It was Eric. Holding a gun up at Bruno's head. A room full of guns were directed at Eric – Eric, who had found his girlfriend and faced the leader of the English Hearts.

Good man!

Jack smiled proudly. Even though he barely knew him, Eric had come across as severely lacking in confidence, unable to conjure the guts to enter such conflict.

Jack had been proven wrong.

"He's a civilian," Jack answered. "His name is Eric."

"What is he doing?" Anders shrugged.

"He's... he's saving his girlfriend, Lieutenant."

Anders lifted his gun and took aim.

"Bruno Tug is too far away to get a shot," Anders instructed his men. "We could fire, but we can't be sure we'd make it. Then he'd flee and we'd have nothing."

"What about Eric?"

Ander's face scrunched up into a repulsed mess. "What do you mean, what about Eric?"

Jack sighed. This was a ridiculous idea, but what the hell. It had been that kind of day.

"What if we give Eric a chance? He's pointing a gun directly at Bruno Tug."

"And how do you suppose we do that?"

"Shoot into the crowd. We'll get some of them, they will disperse, they will stop pointing the gun at Eric. That will give him the chance to pull the trigger."

Anders peered down at Eric, contemplating the idea. Even

from this distance, Eric looked a meek figure. Submissive in nature, with a posture that indicated a clear lack of confidence.

Could they really rely on this man?

"And what if he doesn't?" Anders directed toward Jack, skepticism painted all over his voice.

Jack sighed. Shrugged.

What could he say to that?

It was a risk. No doubt about it, it was not a perfect plan. But the whole situation was far from ideal.

"Have a little faith," Jack replied. "I believe he can do it."

Anders sighed, turning to his squadron, who looked to him for direction.

"Okay, let's do it. Fire into the surrounding crowd," he directed at his squad, who immediately panned out across the balcony, gaining different angles from which to shoot. Anders then turned to Jack. "I hope you're right."

Turning to look at Eric shaking below, Jack nodded.

"Me too."

Jack took aim.

As did the rest of the soldiers.

"Ready. In three."

Jack poised his finger over the trigger.

"Two."

He took in a deep breath.

"One."

Pressing his finger down and holding it in place, he projected his ammunition in a melee of bullets, all directed at the surrounding onlookers of the scene below.

CHAPTER FIFTY-ONE

Eric's body convulsed in a sudden jump.

As if he wasn't tense enough, bullets were now raining down upon the scene.

But not at him.

So he held his arm out strong, a firm grip remaining on the trigger.

He glanced upwards.

Jack.

Yes!

The crowd surrounding him dispersed, taking cover, firing back at the reinforcements above.

This left Bruno, Pearson, Suniya, and Eric in a deadly stalemate.

Eric's arm grew stronger. His fear failed him.

No more guns pointed at him.

This was it. It would all end here.

He may die.

Then again, I may not.

"Tell your man to take the weapon away from her neck," Eric demanded of Bruno, his voice growing stronger.

"Tell your boyfriend to take his gun off my man Bruno," Pearson replied, grinning pathetically at Suniya.

The sound of bullets sent Eric's ears ringing. It was a surround sound storm of terror, a scene like he had never heard before, something that he should find terrifying.

But he didn't care if he died anymore.

He only cared if Suniya lived.

He went deaf to it. The bullets melted away into a vacant murmur. Whilst they attacked his ear with savage intensity, his brain refused to process them. It was nothing.

White noise.

It was him and Bruno.

"What is your name?" Bruno enquired nonchalantly.

"My name has nothing to do with this."

"I was just wanting to know who it is who's so prepared to kill me."

"... Eric."

Eric abruptly regretted imparting this information.

"Ah, Eric. Lovely British name. Tell me this, Eric. What will you do next time there is a terrorist attack?"

Eric scoffed.

"Cry about it," he sarcastically sputtered.

"Exactly. Cry. Never do anything about it. And you dare to challenge me?"

"*How are you any better?*" Eric cried out, his throat hurting with the blades of his screaming anger.

Bruno put his hand out in a calming manner and edged toward Eric.

"I am defending us. Defending this country. From these people who come here to take it from us. How can you not see that?"

"Don't come any closer."

"*How can you not see that?*" Bruno's calm, negotiable

demeanour fell and his intimidating scream caused far more damage than the ringing of the bullets.

"Stay where you are."

Bruno edged closer, his arm lifted out.

"How can you live with it? With 9/11? With 7/7? Innocent people! *How can you live with it?*"

Bruno edged closer.

He was one large pace away.

Eric's hands trembled.

"When people kill in the name of Muslims, and you are fucking one?"

"They don't represent every Muslim."

"They still read the same fucking book!"

Bruno was now one step away from Eric's gun.

He was nearly able to reach it. One quick swipe and Bruno would have the gun off him, and all would be lost.

I need to fire it. I need to do this.

"And you ask how I'm different – I'm killing in the name of protecting us! *I am protecting us!* How the *fuck* can you *live* with *yourself?*"

Eric itched his finger over the trigger.

Got to do this now.

Come on, Eric.

Not a time to be a coward.

Not a time to run away as Suniya gets dragged to her death.

Not a time to leave the student union because he's intimidated by a bunch of laughing blokes on the table next to him.

Not a time to run away from the bathroom because two men question his relationship.

Not a time to give in.

"Tell me, Eric," Bruno smirked, "are you really going to shoot that gun?"

Eric screamed.

A shot fired out.

His finger rested heavily against the trigger he had just pressed.

Bruno's body fell heavily to the floor.

Eric's arms shook.

He had just done it.

He had just killed a man.

CHAPTER FIFTY-TWO

When people get fatally wounded, they usually don't feel the pain, at first.

Bruno had heard stories of people who had been stabbed or shot feeling a delayed onset of agony. They always said it felt like a discomfort. Like it didn't start hurting until they looked down and saw the blood seeping out of their wound.

That such an extreme blow to the chest would knock you onto your back, and you wouldn't completely register at first.

Those people were talking shit.

It caned. Bruno had never felt such tremendous bouts of throbbing pain.

The worst part of it was looking down at his chest, at the open hole in his torso, knowing the bullet had struck such a vital organ as his heart that there was no way he could survive.

That moment of agonising realisation hurt the most. That moment of irrefutable pain shooting up and down your body, your arm spasming as your heart stopped, the indescribable angst at feeling the life seep right out of you – that hurt.

In his mind, he could feel himself slipping away.

Once he registered what was happening, the room turned into a distant blur.

The gunshots grew louder, yet more distant. The ringing in his ears was far away, yet inside his brain. The overwhelming blurriness as his vision failed to scan the distant ceiling, blotches spreading across his immediate sight.

As he coughed, choking up blood, his body seized. Convulsing with such aggressive jolts, it hurt very little – as his body was mostly numb. But he felt the seizure, as his body began to let go of life.

Nearby shouting rang out vaguely in his head.

"Target is down!"

"Confirmed, a bullet to the chest."

"Potteries is secure."

"That's Eric, don't shoot, he's the one who got him."

"Send in the army. We're ready."

Send in the army?

We're ready?

But the army was told not to come in, on the punishment of death.

As his head dropped heavily to the ground, his vision unmasked to reveal his final moments.

A vast sea of dead bodies lay beside him. Masked members of his organisation, splattered with death.

Boots trampling past him. An army uniform of a few men mixing into a dark-green blur that turned to blackness.

It had gone dark.

He could see nothing else.

He could smell burning. Not fire burning; rather, the burning of a hundred rounds of bullets that had landed on the floor.

He could taste iron. A vague sense of blood.

Then all that was left was his hearing.

Distant shouts of triumphant glory from voices he didn't recognise.

Sharnelle.

What were they going to tell Sharnelle?

Soya and Stacey were going to have to grow up without a dad.

He wished it hadn't come to this.

He wished he hadn't perished.

Stacey.

Soya.

My girls.

My family.

My life.

He could hear their distant laughter growing closer, wounding him, growing louder and louder until it was thumping hard against his ear drum.

Sharnelle's threatening voice told them to be quiet.

Daddy needs to sleep now.

His wife.

What would happen next?

And with that, his hearing went.

His final thought ended.

CHAPTER FIFTY-THREE

Once she had released her hands from her restraints, Suniya fell to the floor in a manic weep. Her wrists were bruised a dark grey and throbbed with pain. But she didn't care.

She just didn't care.

She wasn't this person. She wasn't a weak, fretting damsel. She had never needed to be saved.

She stopped crying. Her head slowly rose with eyes full of malice, loathing in her heart, revenge consuming her mind.

Pearson had dropped his knife to the floor.

He was in a solitary heap, unarmed.

She surveyed the room, spotting dead bodies fallen to the floor, with the occasionally surrendering body with their hands on their head.

No one in the English Hearts could spot her.

Six men, five of whom were dressed in army gear, pointed their guns at Pearson.

"You are under arrest," declared the one who wasn't dressed in army gear.

No.

Suniya grabbed hold of the knife Pearson had dropped and

ripped it through the sky to Pearson's throat. She lunged it forward and held it there, poised, less than an inch from taking his life.

Her glare intensified.

Everything he had done.

He deserved to die.

"Put the knife down," instructed a voice from nearby.

Suniya ignored it.

Pearson looked back at her. He grinned. He still grinned, even after he was caught, arrested, potentially at the end of his life – he still grinned.

It infuriated her.

"Put it down!" came another shout.

They weren't going to shoot her. Surely.

Not to stop her killing the bastard who had done this to her.

Her eye contact remained on his. Intensifying. Haphazardly concentrated.

She was no one's to be rescued.

He had abused her. Tortured her. *Humiliated her*.

She did not let anybody treat her like that.

"Suniya."

It was a familiar voice.

"Suniya, please."

A loving hand cushioned her shoulder. She didn't flinch it off. She kept it. Enjoyed it. Allowed its contact to meet her skin.

"Put the knife down, Suniya, please," begged Eric's voice, close to her ear.

Suniya's hand gripped tighter.

"I am *not* like *you*," she venomously spat at Pearson's smirking face. "And that is the only reason you get to live."

The knife clattered to the floor with an almighty reverb.

The men who Suniya assumed had come to her rescue burst

forward, grabbing hold of Pearson, throwing him to the floor, fastening his hands into restraints.

Suniya turned her back to it and dove into Eric's arms. Every emotion she had fought, bottled up and buried for the previous hours burst out.

She collapsed, falling into Eric, taking him to the ground. Eric tried to steady her but couldn't, and had no choice but to fall to his knees with her. Despite the difficulty in keeping her up, his arms did not leave her for a second. They stayed wrapped around her, surrounding her in a warmth of comfort.

Laying on his knees, he held her as her tears streamed like bullets. Her fists clenched Eric's shirt, clasping it in her hands, gripping onto him.

"It's okay, Suniya," Eric whispered in her ear. "It's over. I'm here, it's okay."

She lifted her head to meet his eyes. She could see her emotional state almost break him, pained by witnessing her distress, so she willed it away. Propping herself up on her arm, she stroked a gentle hand down the side of his face.

"You were so brave," she told him. "You were so, so brave. I'm so proud of you."

A smile grew. Forcing itself through the complexity of her anxious state, it grew, lifting his spirits as it did.

"You were so, so good. Thank you. Thank you for saving me."

"Of course," Eric replied. "Did you really think I could just leave you?"

Suniya shook her head, stifling tears once more.

No. I didn't.

Eric helped Suniya to her feet and, keeping an arm propped around her, helped her limp forward. Her wounds were still raw, but they would heal in time.

"Eric," came the voice of the man Eric would later tell

Suniya about – a police officer called Jack Taylor. A hero, and the inspiration Eric had needed

"Jack," Eric answered.

Suniya watched Eric and Jack share a moment of silent contemplation, which grew into a smile, which grew into a laugh.

"Did your family get out okay?" Eric inquired.

"Yes. And now Bruno Tug is down, and the army has entered the city. Thanks to you."

Jack stuck out a hand and Eric took it, shaking it firmly.

"This is Suniya," Eric pointed out. "My girlfriend."

"You've got a brilliant man as a boyfriend, Suniya."

"Yes," confirmed Suniya. "Yes, I do."

CHAPTER FIFTY-FOUR

Eric gently kissed Suniya's head.

Her head lulled and sank against his shoulder, her eyes closing. She was finally sleeping.

It was about time.

The experience had been exhausting. The follow-up questions, the psychiatrists, the hospital treatment. It had taken days for them to finally get home.

But there they were.

Sat on the sofa, snuggly nestled in front of the television.

Finally at peace.

Not wanting to wake her, Eric turned the volume on the television down. The news headlines were still reporting on the atrocities that had happened, and with more and more that was revealed, the more shocking it became.

Then the prime minister came on to address the nation.

Eric listened intently to their words.

"Many have said that these events were unprecedented," the prime minister announced. "Yes. They were. But we need to look inwardly, look at events in this country, in this world, and ask ourselves — was it unprecedented? Or, was it that no one picked up on it?"

The prime minister took in a deep breath, looked at the assembled media, and continued.

"Wise words," Eric spoke softly to himself.

With a weak smile at the sound of Suniya's deep breathing, he too closed his eyes, rested his head on hers, and drifted off to sleep.

As he did, the words of the prime minister seeped from the television and into his sleeping mind.

"All this time, we were fearing what came from foreign soil. We never saw how that fear could destroy us from within."

AUTHOR'S NOTE

When writing this novel, I was always worried about the violence and controversial subject matter. Whether it would be taken in the right way.

Whether depicting such awful acts toward minorities was too close to potential reality, and whether this made it too upsetting, especially considering current events.

Then, I realised it should be upsetting.

Look at the world around you.

Racism is rising to power in some of the most powerful countries in the world.

I hope this novel serves as a stark reminder of what happens when these horrendous views aren't challenged.

You do have a voice. Use it.

Rick

GET TWO BOOKS FOR FREE

Join Rick's Reader's Group at **www.rickwoodwriter.com** for two of his books :

SOME BOOKS AVAILABLE BY RICK WOOD...

RICK WOOD

SHUTTER HOUSE

This Book Is Full Of Bodies

Rick Wood

RICK WOOD

THE ART OF MURDER

SEAN MALLON BOOK ONE

RICK WOOD

CIA ROSE BOOK ONE

AFTER THE DEVIL HAS WON

RICK WOOD

ROSES ARE RED SO IS YOUR BLOOD

BLOOD SPLATTER BOOKS

18+

PSYCHO
B*TCHES

Rick Wood

www.ingramcontent.com/pod-product-compliance
Ingram Content Group UK Ltd.
Pitfield, Milton Keynes, MK11 3LW, UK
UKHW041506301125
9275UKWH00033B/526